Endorsements

David Boyer, MD   Psychiatrist

The New Old Testament made me think about so many things that are intrinsically meaningful to me that, by the time I was finished, I felt like a better person. I can't think of any deeper impact that a book could make.

Judy Wax-Goldwasser   Writer

Cary, I finally had the time to give your manuscript the time that I felt it deserved, and I'm totally bowled over. It's absolutely marvelous. I am SO impressed with your creativity, knowledge base, writing and humor. You MUST get it published—and I want a first edition. A book like this could really catch on with the right publisher and promotional approach. BRAVO!!!! GET IT PUBLISHED!!!!! It's brilliant, creative and unique. What more could one want?

Marilyn Green   Elementary School Teacher

I owe you one big apology. I started your bible shortly after you sent it to me. Adored the beginning and put it aside…Anyway, two weeks later, I printed out the entire book and could NOT put it down. LOVED IT, LOVED IT.

Joe Nessim   Activist

I loved the opening quotations and was very intrigued by some including Pope Pius IX and of course Jerry Falwell. But most of all, I have to say that you have put into words, feelings that I have had for many years.

Helen Goldberg   Escapee from the Holocaust/Optometrist

Your approach is humane. We may not be ready for it now, but just as the 20ᵗʰ Century brought drastic changes, let us hope the 21ˢᵗ Century will usher in a time of harmony, respect and brotherhood among nations as you envision. You must publish your work.

Becky Sherlock   Artist

I just finished reading your book. Your writing has hit and inspired new thoughts + beginning for me. I really feel you were inspired to write this. Your words flow and I feel good reading them…Your lines "Freedom will not be a gift from Me unto thee but an achievement of your mind and your soul…" The whole lesson here makes so much sense. We are responsible for ourselves—not to ask God to do these things for us…it is so good.

THE
NEW OLD
TESTAMENT

CARY J. STEGMAN

⌐ ARCHWAY
PUBLISHING

Archway Publishing books may be ordered through booksellers or by contacting:

Archway Publishing
1663 Liberty Drive
Bloomington, IN 47403
www.archwaypublishing.com
1 (888) 242-5904

ISBN: 978-1-4808-1865-1 (sc)
ISBN: 978-1-4808-1866-8 (hc)
ISBN: 978-1-4808-1867-5 (e)

Library of Congress Control Number: 2015909883

Print information available on the last page.

Archway Publishing rev. date: 07/14/2015

Cover Illustration

The cover illustration and the image above are derivative graphics built upon Michelangelo's Sistine Chapel ceiling fresco, "The Creation of Adam."

The object behind God in the original fresco is credibly a stylized artistic representation of a near-midline saggital section of the human brain. In this derived image, Michelangelo's stylized brain has been replaced with a near-midline saggital section of the human brain symbolizing the gift of REASON, the precious treasure of human intellect, being bestowed onto mankind.

In the original fresco, the tips of the index fingers of God and Adam are touching. Instead, in this image, the index fingers gently touch a fracturing egg, a vessel, an Ark containing a creation. The cracking egg emitting cataclysmic forces is a visual metaphor of the Big Bang. The energy bursting forth symbolizes the birth of the universe, of humanity, of all living things, of intellect and its scientific and technological progeny as well as the nucleus of the atom and stars creating the cosmos. Thus, observe across the starry firament, scientific and mathematical equations as well as cells of early human and animal embryologic development.

ἐν ἀρχῇ ἦν ὁ λόγος καὶ ὁ λόγος ἦν πρὸς
τὸν θεόν καὶ θεὸς ἦν ὁ λόγο

John 1:1
Original Greek Text

In the beginning was the Word, and the Word
was with God, and the Word was God.

John 1:1
Translation in the King James New Testament

Alternative translation:

In the beginning was Reason, and Reason was
with God, and Reason was God.

Consider the potential vast consequences of replacing
"the Word" with "Reason" an alternative translation
of the Greek "logos" found in the original text.

c. j. stegman

Credo quia absurdum (I believe because it is absurd)."

Tertullian
Circa: 200AD

"Even though faith is above reason, there can never be any real disagreement between faith and reason ... God cannot deny himself, nor can truth ever be in opposition to truth ... Therefore we define that every assertion contrary to the truth of enlightened faith is totally false. Hence all faithful Christians are forbidden to defend as the legitimate conclusions of science those opinions which are known to be contrary to the doctrine of faith, particularly if they have been condemned by the church; and furthermore they are absolutely bound to hold them to be errors which wear the deceptive appearance of truth."

Pope Pius IX
First Vatican Council
1869-1870

So as shown by the quotes above, theologians have visited unto generations, the concept that the more absurd an accepted precept, the more fervent is your faith and therefore the more profound your belief system, even if in total opposition to the observable reality of the world! How profoundly absurd! The preposterous has been a metaphysical inoculation against reason that for centuries upon centuries has confounded and besieged the domain of science. Even today, we still drown in a sea, a tsunami, of ignorant belief in which some modern theologians and jurists, powerful theologians and jurists, believing that they know the WORD, that they know God's mind and motives, unabashedly make detestable irrational pronouncements. The following statements regarding 9/11, the Indian Sea Tsunami and the divine derivation of governmental authority allowing the power of revenge (not justice) as well as wrath by the sword (might is right … almighty is always right) indicate a philosophical viewpoint that should be viewed as demeaning to an almighty being and disturbing to thoughtful individuals.

From Pat Robertson and Jerry Falwell are comments about 9/11 …

"I do believe, as a theologian, based upon many Scriptures and particularly Proverbs 14:23, which says 'living by God's principles promotes a nation to greatness, violating those principles brings a nation to shame.'" Organizations "which have attempted to secularize America, have removed our nation from its relationship with Christ on which it was founded. I therefore believe that that created an environment which possibly has caused God to lift the veil of protection which has allowed no one to attack America on our soil since 1812."

> Pat Robertson
> September 2001
> Regarding 9/11

"I really believe that the pagans, and the abortionists, and the feminists, and the gays and the lesbians who are actively trying to make that an alternative lifestyle, the ACLU, People For the American Way, all of them who have tried to secularize America. I point the finger in their face and say 'you helped this happen.'"

> Jerry Falwell
> September 2001
> Regarding 9/11

and from the head of Indonesia' Council of Clerics come these remarks about the devastating tsunami of 2004 ...

"Allah will not love us without also testing our love for him. Maybe this disaster was because we have forgotten him and his teachings and failed to implement [Islamic] Shariah law."

Din Syamsuddin
Head; Indonesia's Council of Clerics
Regarding Tsunami
1/8/2005

... and finally from Antonin Scalia ...

"...government, however you want to limit that concept, derives its moral authority from God. It is the minister of God with powers to revenge, to execute wrath, including wrath by the sword ..."

Antonin Scalia
Justice, United States Supreme Court
Pew Conference on Capital Punishment
January 25, 2002

So even today, theological delusion, superstition and intolerance color policy decisions and interpretation of causation of current events. Now read the following quotes that grow out of rational and analytic worldviews. Herein lies the basic theme of this book.

"He from whom nothing is hidden created me and I have all measure in me both of what is heavenly above and what is earthly and infernal. And who understands himself understands much."

Mariano di Jacopo aka Taccola "the Crow" (1382-c.1453)

"It is setting a high value upon our opinions to roast men and women alive on account of them."

Michel de Montaigne (1533-1592), French essayist and philosopher

---

"Whenever we read the obscene stories, the voluptuous debaucheries, the cruel and tortuous executions, the unrelenting vindictiveness, with which more than half the Bible is filled it would be more consistent that we call it the word of a demon than the word of God. It is a history of wickedness that has served to corrupt and brutalize."

Thomas Paine, The Age of Reason (1792)

"The case my friend is that the world has been over-run with fable and creeds of human invention, with sectaries of whole nations against all other nations, and sectaries of those sectaries in each of them against the other. Every sectary, except the Quakers, had been a persecutor. Those who fled from persecution persecuted in turn, and it is this that has filled the world with persecution and deluged it with blood."

Thomas Paine
Letter to John Adam

"The truths of religion are never so well understood as by those who have lost the power of reasoning."

Voltaire
1694-1778

————————————

"The whole scheme of Christian Salvation is diabolical as revealed by the creeds. An angry God, imagine such a creator of the universe. Angry at what he knew was coming and was himself responsible for. Then he sets himself about to beget a son, in order that the child should beg him to forgive the Sinner. This however he cannot or will not do. He must punish somebody—so the son offers himself up & our creator punishes the innocent youth, never heard of before—for the guilty and became reconciled to us. ... I decline to accept Salvation from such a fiend."

Andrew Carnegie, to Sir James Donaldson,
Principal of St. Andrews University
June 1, 1905.
Letters (except to Haldane) in Library of Congress collection,
cited by Joseph Frazier Wall, Andrew Carnegie, 1970.

————————————

"A man's behavior should be based effectually on sympathy, education and social ties and needs. I believe there is nothing divine about morality. It is a purely human affair but the most important of all human affairs."

Albert Einstein
Raymond Swing's CBS program "This I Believe"
Circa 1954
Quote provided by the Albert Einstein Archives
at the Hebrew University of Jerusalem

I am God ... Dogma I

Palindrome
c. j. stegman

Nature and nature's laws lay hid in night,
God said Let Newton be! And all was light.

Alexander Pope
Epitaph intended for Sir Isaac Newton

And as science illuminates the Laws of Nature
and God's nature with Light;
Fanatics of faith cast a shadow of darkness
dooming mankind to endless Night.

With apologies to Alexander Pope
c. j. stegman

If Revelations in the New Testament is divinely
authored ... then Stephen King may be God.

c. j. stegman

Preface

In the beginning, I began writing in order to put into proper perspective, as I perceived it, a story that had haunted me since childhood—the story of God commanding Abraham to sacrifice his son, Isaac. As a cornerstone of Jewish theology, this story had scared me, a child, out of belief in that God—that God who would test Abraham by requiring a deed so hideously immoral. How could a father, any loving father, bow to His will and unquestioningly obey God in such a wicked, albeit, unexecuted act?

And as I grew, so did the questions. Was this not the amoral manipulation of an insecure, faithless despotic God? What might Abraham potentially have known of this God? That conduct failing His morally ambiguous expectations and divine statutes, as yet undeclared, brought His swift relentless vengeful punishment! That He had wielded flood and conflagration indiscriminately with totalitarian brutality. Was Abraham's acceptance, his complicity, an act of faith, an act of trust, a cognitive act based on thoughtful theodicy or an act based on the desire to survive, of rational fear— for did he not have reason to fear Him? Or was Abraham mistaken? For how would he have known if he was hearing God or the Devil? Or a disingenuous God with the duplicitous two-faced physiognomy of Janus: beneficent ... malicious ... both! Was this "moral hazard" fashioned by this all-powerful entity subjugating this man and his future nation into submission to divine power, creating a collective consciousness of fatalism, a covenant of dependency, seducing them, leading them to their recurring self-sacrifice upon the altar of history? Why does an all-powerful being need validation by the bellicose "shock and awe" display of the violence of His power? Is the implicit message one of blind obedience to God's will? That obedience might bring Godly rewards, if only the staying of His terrifying castigating hand. And if so, if He does not speak directly to us but through "divine" or divinely inspired imprecise text, who interprets His will … fanatic religious clerics offering heaven for terrorist acts … fundamentalist zealots with temporal power and biblical justification for torturing and murdering heretics, apostates and non-believers in order to bring them to revelation … to the way of Truth? Men of faith have wielded weapons of fire and water, slavery and terror, brutality and torture, war and hate, heaven and hell in the name of God. And so we are taught … and so it is indelibly etched into the psyches of many … that reacting with vengeful cruel overwhelming authoritarian power and violence is the Godly sanctioned course, the final solution, rather than thoughtful empathic kindness and justice as the divine path. So it was … so it is.

And more than a millennium later, the story was refashioned, reworked, to its sacrificial conclusion by the bearing of a Cross across the theological abyss from the jealous vengeful vigilante God of the Old Testament to the prolicidal "loving" God of the New Testament. And more concerns. How can humanity accept a God who prescribes sacrifice of the innocent to test devotion and faithfulness; and concomitantly as expiation for the sins of sinners? And why do Isaac and Jesus, innocent Isaac and Jesus, acquiesce to their imminent sacrifice? How can such an odious story be a cornerstone of two major western religions? From Isaac to Jesus can be seen the devolution of the Judeo-Christian "epic" from salvation by affirmation of life to salvation through the avowal of death. And how can one consider spiritually gratifying a Father of infinite wisdom and unlimited power, choosing torture and death, abuse and cruelty, in execution of His "virtuous" son by His powerless "actors," his marionettes, constrained, preordained, to play the roles He had scripted on His omniscient oft virtue-less stage? Should He not use His potential for infinite compassion and compelling instruction? How does the evil death of innocents bring death to evil? What does this violent divinely arranged execution teach mankind? Is it not the penultimate evil to sadistically sacrifice an innocent being as absolution for the evils of the guilty? Why is it that Good Friday is good? And sadly, this "divinely" inspired and orchestrated scenario creates a legacy of scapegoats. Jesus, the sacrificial "goat," "lamb," dies, but does not really die, for the sins of others; and the Jews become scapegoats for his "murder," condemned to drown in rivers of blood, filled with hate, for millennia ... to this very day. Do we sacrifice our own intuitive understanding of righteousness by accepting these despicable acts, enslaving our reason to a morbid sense of redemption via blind faith? And truly, is this sacrifice not a sacrifice at all? Would it have unfolded without preordained orchestration by God? And how would it be possible that God would not know the outcome? That in reality his son (His own incarnation?) was not dying but was being reborn. And why must Jesus suffer sadistic violence ... why the need for torture on the cross? Did the Almighty not have the knowledge or power to "anesthetize" his son? Has God less compassion for his son than human beings, such as Good Samaritans, have for strangers who are suffering? "Power corrupts, absolute power corrupts absolutely." So it seems that divine absolute power corrupts the divine absolutely!

And why does a benevolent God, a loving God, torture us, physically and emotionally, with the knowledge of our inevitable frequently pain-filled death? Made in His image, we are a defective product without warranty and a short shelf life. Through torture of disease and decrepitude are we cleansed, are we purified? Through suffering do we gain unadulterated knowledge that may be our salvation? Does not God have the capability to whisper kindly into our ears, "Warmly embrace those you love, say goodbye, and I will gather you up in my arms so I may cradle you with affection for eternity"?

Yet it is absurd to condemn an unknowable God. For, in truth, we cannot know God unless He gives to Mankind tangible direct substantiation of His existence. Consequently, we neither know whether "He" exists nor whether "He" exists among a pantheon of Gods. Ironically, after all, it is "all-knowing" God who commands, "You shall have no other Gods before Me" therein declaring the existence of more than one God. Therefore, our concern should not be with the existential questions about God but His biblically purported character and deeds. Our distress should rather be with organized religions' debased conceptualization of the divine ... God made in man's image. An oftentimes-hideous Franken-god ... a manmade creation out of control ... fabricated as camouflage for ulterior motives, hidden agendas. For are the holy scriptures really divine or divinely inspired ... or the creation of organized religion acting to manipulate humankind in order to nourish its own institutional craving for profit, power and glory?

Furthermore, if He created us in His own image, why are we not perfect—perfect physically and spiritually? Certainly, this is not the case. Is the imperfection of our creation His choice or His failure? Men strive for perfection in their creations, falling short. If omnipotent, why would He accept less than perfection? Why would He not infallibly create perfection? Alternatively, if He purposefully made humankind imperfect, then why His bewilderment and malevolent reaction to humanity's imperfect deeds? Is it not "cruel to make the fault and punish it too"? Thus, is humankind a reflection of His imperfection? Who then created whom? God is perfect and forever. Man is imperfect and ephemeral. God can do no wrong because his actions, whether good or evil, judged by human standards are protected in mists of mystery. But should not human intelligence and intuition born in the essence of human introspection and interaction, empathy and compassion, penetrate the mystery? Could Abraham, a creation of "God," not intuitively understand the immorality of God's command to sacrifice his son? Can an almighty God … omniscient … omnipotent … omnipresent … immortal … ever truly experience human emotions from the deep abyss of human suffering to the pinnacle of human joy? And, therefore know on the human scale … right and wrong? God cannot stand at "the flaming forge of life" for His fortunes are boundless, manipulated by his own almighty caprice, transformed at whim. While the fortunes of men are forever wrought by "each burning deed and thought."

Surely, the story of Isaac has also been problematic to others … to many. I felt deeply that this story could be retold, must be retold, because of the disturbing implications in its traditional telling. I desired to recount the story so that Abraham, and also God, by my perception, would be moral and benevolent figures, guided by compassion, teaching ethics and character, rather than participating in this profligate scenario as it unfolds in the Bible.

So in the retelling, commentary was intentionally avoided. For centuries, scholarly scriptural interpretation has been written in an attempt to harvest from these "holy" bad seeds a crop of good deeds. But commentary is not an intellectual alchemy resulting in transmutation of base text into golden holy revelation. If substantially, the base, the foundation, of "divine" scripture is intrinsically corrupt then could it truly be divinely inspired? And if human commentary seeks righteousness from the base, from the immoral, then who is divine? Is it not offensive to man and God to have to seek for good in evil, especially in the context of religious narrative? Is it not potentially dangerous? Does not the Bible provide, has not the Bible provided, for many individuals and organizations/institutions, both political and religious, validation of the malevolent element in human nature? Cannot the "bad," the wicked in our psyche, find justification …

compulsion ... even egocentric salvation, in committing malevolent acts analogous to those of God and the patriarchs as told in stories attributed to be His word? Could any reasonable individual subscribe to commentaries affirming the Holocaust as a divine revelatory event meant to teach mankind ethics and morality—should that not be considered outrageous—despicable?

My rewriting of the story of Abraham and Isaac was meant only for my own edification and gratification. This goal being achieved, I thought I had reached an end. However, after my wife, Shirley, and at her suggestion, our dearest friends, had read it, they urged me to continue to rewrite other biblical stories, stories that had bothered them also. So from an intended limited beginning, this creation, this manuscript, began to grow, drawing me down new paths through the Bible. And it was only with their encouragement and love, for which I will always be profoundly grateful, that I have been able to trudge along.

And in doing so, as an allopathic physician committed to medical practice based on scientific method, I found myself traveling a divergent path—a path I had traveled before, but had not, on previous wanderings, explored as deeply. This path straddled a hazardous route astride a fault line, a rift, where the ostensibly opposing tectonic plates of science and faith, of the factual and the spiritual, of knowledge and religion collide. Science and faith, so often discordant, have produced social entropy. When scientific theory and technological progress refute absolutist infallible religious conviction, or contrarily, when religious conviction obstructs development of science and technology, the dominion of each is assaulted. Thus historically and contemporaneously, the controversy of the quest for zero and the polemics of Atomists and Aristotelians, heliocentricism and geocentricism, evolutionary theory and creationism, genetic intervention and God's magisteria of "inheritance" are but a few examples of the conflicts of these domains. Does the burning bright spirit of scientific inquiry so profoundly intimidate and challenge people of faith compelling them to burn at the stake, literally and figuratively, the perceived transgressors and their heretical transgression? Yet despite these conflicts, the inquisitive scientific mind is compulsively driven to seek understanding of the physical world. Albert Einstein was once asked, "What is the most powerful force in the universe?" His answer, "compound interest." And so it is that the compounded interest of scientists building upon the capital of predecessors has exponentially and miraculously grown the principles of science profiting mankind with wondrous technological benefits. So driven, scientific explorers of the macro-cosmos and micro-cosmos, while pursuing their quest, may step into ... stumble down ... a white rabbit's black hole or into worm-holes where they grasp at enigmatic yet energetic strings in an attempt to guide their fall into multiple mathematically deduced inconceivable ineffable dimensions, Black Holes of arguable oblivion or the forever of the endless infinitesimal and the endless infinite ... the infinitesimal something and infinite something balanced on the fulcrum of nothing (zero). And alas, they drift downward into a wonderland "observed" through the scientific looking glass ... a looking glass magnifying the dimensions of our universe beyond those merely observable. And also peering into the micro-cosmos of subatomic particles as well as M-theory (M=membrane, magic, mystery), parallel membranes (meme-brain universes/cultures) and the macro-cosmos of dark energy in each of which the creation of something from nothing as well as nothing from something is hypothesized to be a physical reality. And so, amazingly and unexpectedly, as modern scientific theory and knowledge, as concepts of zero and infinity, time and space, general relativity and quantum mechanics (something from nothing) are contemplated and perhaps reconciled, mankind is drawn into new dimensions—new dimensions beyond the boundaries of human comprehension—a great leap from the physical domain into an ostensible metaphysical magisterium. Walking this path, I felt compelled to attempt, as feeble as it might be, to bring these seemingly antithetical, adversarial, themes into a harmony, blending diverse perspectives into a symphonic whole praising the wonders of creation.

The wonders of creation, of the natural world, stimulate men to quest for scientific knowledge. This quest is limited only by the expanse of their intellect and is set free by the depth of their faith—a very particular faith. For the men and women of science must have faith that the workings of the universe are universal and that nature can be understood as well as codified into a valid and utilizable body of knowledge. And they must have faith that the workings of nature are unchanging, immutable, unified. If not, if by the caprice of a supernatural hand these can be altered, turned topsy-turvy at whim, then knowledge would be unfruitful, transitory and futile. Equally important, scientists must have faith in the scientific method. When scientific investigation and theory lead to counter-intuitive, counter-experiential, countercultural and counter-theological concepts, scientists must have faith and not abandon their quest of discovery. For instance, when time is found to vary with speed contradicting experience, when dimensions expand beyond the four we can understand challenging our world perception, when the theory of evolution tests for some their self image, faith in the scientific method must trump common conventional or religious sensibilities and sensitivities in the empirical domain. And it must be understood that no scientific law or theory is absolutely verifiable and, more importantly, each and every law and theory can always, potentially, be falsifiable … disproved by observation or experimentation. Neither condition is applicable to religious faith for this faith is not accountable to the discernable natural world. Neither has standing in organized religion for Nature's court is irrelevant to these institutions. So, for instance, the story of the creation of man as modified from its biblical roots in this book is not to be misconstrued as support for the concept of intelligent design which can neither be proven true nor, more significantly, false. Perhaps God's formula for humankind's quest is $E=mc^2$: Enlightenment equals Marvel times Conceptualization times Conviction in scientific method. Faith is therefore at the foundation of the scientific quest. In this sense faith and knowledge are partners. And the scientist's bible is the credo of his faith—a faith rewarded by advances in human knowledge and technology—moving man closer to "heaven" on earth when used wisely and morally.

The scientist's Bible is composed of the Book of Observation—the Genesis of Ideas created by wonder. The Book of Hypotheses—the attempted Exodus from ignorance into the "promised" land of knowledge. The Book of Empiric Codes—-the rules and methods, the Leviticus, the established "priestly" conventions by which measurable and repeatable empiric data is obtained by testing the natural world proving or disproving a postulated premise. The Book of Analysis of Results—-the principles by which Numbers, the data, are appropriately and impartially analyzed. And lastly, the Book of Natural Laws, a covenant of understanding of the "truth" of the natural world—the Deuteronomy (Due-to-astronomy) of "proven" hypotheses—-revealed by human intellect using scientific method. And most astoundingly and beneficially, another book—the Book of Prophets (profits)—giving birth to man's modern identity and myriad human technological advances. Full of wonder ... fraught with potential horror ... humankind is innately compelled to explore the tree of knowledge in order to attain a lusty bite from the Apple (Adam's, Newton's, Steve Job's) ... for good ... or, unfortunately, evil. So it is by this good book that Nature's God and Man, constrained by natural laws, are seekers of knowledge and faith. "Strong in will ... to strive, to seek, to find, and not to yield." For each searches for the infinite, where humankind's knowledge reaches God's faith—God's spirit. And the ontological quest of human spirituality is equaled by the expansive nature of human intellect searching for understanding of the workings of the cosmos.

But faith must be treated carefully for it can be a blinding obstructive misleading force extinguishing the enlightenment of reason and entombing evidence-based tenets in darkness. The advancement of science must not be lost, overwritten, in a palimpsest* of ignorance and religious text. For the faith of many teaches that the truth divinely revealed is the "truth" even when contradicted by "Truth" competently determined by scientific observation and method. Does God work in mysterious ways not to be known by man? Or are God's mysterious ways his means to compel men to explore creation and discover its secrets ... secrets perhaps also unknown to Him? For if known by Him, why would He not have shared them in divine text enriching and saving lives? Are the laws of nature obfuscated to create the perception of an omnipotent power? Or does that omnipotent power desire that we embrace our "God-given" intellect and the challenges He, or rather Nature, have placed before us so that commonly held experience and knowledge of our shared worlds will bind us deeply—a divine universality? Is this not the greatest blessing? Is it not our quintessential destiny? Is it not an appropriate, an honorable, an inherent "hubris" of our spirit?

Through this quest mankind has profited. Not just by the knowledge gained and technological advances, but also by the values and ethics which scientists have come to recognize are essential in the search for understanding of natural phenomena sought by the scientific process. Science is indifferent to morality. But scientific method can only be efficacious when captive to the highest moral standards. Meticulous honesty in research (ritual) and strict adherence to an ethical code (commandments) are imperative with peer review providing "religious" enforcement. It is fundamental that the "religion" of

---

* Palimpsest: A book or manuscript on which the original text has been bleached out but of which shadows remain and new text is over-written, frequently perpendicular to the original writing. Palimpsests were primarily artifacts of the Middle Ages when parchment was rare and expensive. The fascinating "Archimedes Palimpsest" can be viewed at: http://www.archimedespalimpsest.org

science be ethical in order to achieve its "theology" of revelation of earthly knowledge and temporal "salvation" of the human condition. When falling short of its principles, the unprincipled are commonly discovered by unfettered peer review or failure to reproduce testable outcomes. Its failures cannot be hidden or lost in a shroud of divine delusions. In failure, knowledge is gained upon which future success can be achieved. Science cannot allow inquisitions meant to coerce individuals to accept the ineffable and inconstant truths of organized religion because the foundation of science is concrete and discoverable truth. Additionally, science aspires to a democratic discourse unlike the authoritarian hierarchy of many organized religions. The values and traits esteemed in the scientific community and considered essential to scientific methodology—rationality, honesty, ethics, open-mindedness, skepticism, hard work, perseverance, joy of discovery and curiosity—apply well beyond the domain of science. It has not always been so.

The Bible, testaments old and new, has profoundly influenced all echelons of human interaction throughout the history of mankind. Unfortunately and incontrovertibly, all too frequently, the "Holy Book" has been an inspiration for unholy acts. Its words, often ambiguous and inconsistent, have been used as justification for commission of horrid offenses—offenses perceived as sanctioned by interpretation of God's presumed words and actions. As God committed genocides, so have the creatures created in His image, disturbingly, on occasion, by God's direct command. When men "institutionalize" God, are they not all too often led into temptation—the temptation to usurp divine power? "Understand that you are God. You have God's capacity of aliveness and sensation and memory and foresight; God's power to rule and govern and direct the body that is your servant, in the same way as God himself, who reigns over us, directs the entire universe." Parenthetically, is not the sectarian paradigm of heaven and hell found in biblical text and religious theology an ultimate weapon of a "crusade" to divide and enslave humankind? What greater crime against humanity than to lay claim to the power of gatekeeper in order to control access to eternal providence? By mundane sectarian fiat and arrogant augury, a powerful ministry in delusion and folly usurps the "keys of the kingdom" for its holy see to extort by parochial ransom—-only sardonically turning the key in the lock to heaven's gates by procuring monetary dispensation or spiritual enslavement. And all too commonly, the self-righteous faithful believers, while professing that the foundation for their probity is biblical morality, take actions and formulate policies which are all too often antithetical to those values. So, is man made in God's image or is the image of God man-made? Is God requisite for human morality? Assuredly, not! What if His words were not subject to interpretation? Why is His Good Book not overflowing with unambiguous GOOD? What if He had acted only out of compassion and benevolence, never with vengeful violence? What if the Bible stated definitively that violence is sin, an unacceptable means of resolution of human conflict? Would world history have been changed? Invoking jingoistic affirmations, "God wills it!" or "God is with us," not only condones Jihad, Crusade, Inquisition, war and many other forms of violence but also anoints each with God's blessing. Soldiers of the same religion but of differing nationality and/or political ideology have killed and maimed each other in numerous wars while clergy in each belligerent camp affirm and encourage this violence because "God is on our side." Does God or should God truly sanctify violence? I am God—dogma I! And so it is that Constantine's Sword—the Cross ... the Crucifix—an instrument created for torture and murder, a device of tyranny—proclaims from steeples on high and as pendants hanging near human hearts; a religion—amongst others—that has a legacy of torture, murder and tyranny. History tells us the story of mankind, a story in which organized bible-avowing religions have abjectly failed to provide the moral, political and societal framework for intercultural, inter-societal and international tolerance, brotherhood, and peace.

I hope that new stories born of old will bring forth new perceptions and, more importantly, fresh approaches to our actions in everyday real life situations. For, as Susan Jacoby writes in her book, <u>Freethinkers</u> (p.52), "at the core of … religion {should} lay not unquestioning faith but a deep reverence for the power of the human mind and the value of human doubt." Perhaps, just perhaps, we, as individuals and the society of humankind, will be more empathic … more compassionate … more humane.

In the beginning …we should begin to create that which will have meaning in the end. And so hopefully it shall be …that we "begin at the beginning and go on until we come to the end, then stop"[1]… in the beginning …

"Where's Waldo?"

Throughout this book are political, theological, philosophical, scientific, cultural and literary references to existing works, some directly quoted are indicated by quotation marks and others modified to fit like pieces of a puzzle into the context of the work are not so designated. Have fun finding these references.

"Waldos" are listed at the end of the book.

בָּרְכוּ אֶת יְיָ הַמְּבֹרָךְ

Transliteration:
Barchu et Ado-nai ha-m'vorach

Translation:
Bless the Lord who is to be praised.

"It Ain't Necessarily So"

Moderato Scherzoso

Words and Music by George Gershwin,
DuBose and Dorothy Heyward and Ira Gershwin

The melody of "It Ain't Necessarily So" is essentially the same as the melody of the above blessing in Hebrew, well known to the Gershwins, which is recited before the reading of the Torah (The Old Testament). Using this melody, as well as the lyrics of the Gershwin song, overtly expressed their religious skepticism.

The First Book of Moses

Genesis

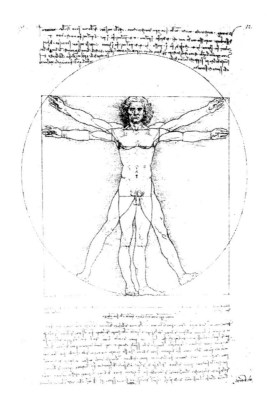

Creation

In the beginning, there was void...black...whole...and within the void was the singularity...the oneness...of the ark, an orb. And within this orb were the infinite ordered mass, energies, time and vitality...the heavenly nucleus... of the nascent universe.

And the gravity of the ark was great...binding God...within.

And God beheld the confining shells of the ark. And He could not restrain His desire to be free...but the bonds were powerful... constraining. And the mass, gravity, and dark energy locked within were all mighty. And so it was.

And God placed His trust in faith, in the Word, for He felt that faith...that the Word...could set Him free. But He was perplexed, for He knew not the unknown Word. And He waited an eternity. And still He was not free. And He was a slave to His faith.

And by faith, despairing at nature's indifference, He realized that His chance for freedom was nil. And He was downcast, for His constrained existence was a Bohr. And bored by everything being nothing, He dreamed of something.

And God thought, *by faith, in bondage, must I abide? Might the power of reason set Me free?*

And so in the beginning was reason. And reason was with God. And God was reason.

With exhilaration, He anticipated the miraculous, for He realized that reason Bohr promise...that out of nothing something may come.

From the nucleus of the Ark, He observed its structure, studying its encompassing shells. And He postulated. He hypothesized. And He tested. And He persevered, finding the way, penetrating the impenetrable shells. And it was so.

And the mass and energy within the Ark were unleashed. And there was a big bang, a cataclysm. And a tempest burst forth betwixt the cracks in the Ark. And the "blastosphere" of the embryonic universe exploded forth…radiating…into randomness and chaos, accelerating and expanding, releasing time and displacing the void. And God by the might of reason was set free…liberated to explore the beauty of the new embryonic elegant universe.

And God was amazed at the energy and mass of the firmament born by the power of His mind, and He wondered if they were good. And it was so.

And God was alarmed. For in the chaos of energy and mass he had wrought, He knew trepidation. In the uncontrolled randomness, He was insecure. Apocalypse encircled Him. And the face of God, buried in tempest, was filled by fear. But unforeseen, the Laws of Nature were liberated upon the chaos molding, modeling, commanding, controlling creation. And He feared no longer. For He acknowledged the essence of the Laws, naked almighty power—the supreme creator. And Nature was exposed, au naturel…its immutable Laws no longer held captive, no longer suspended within the Ark. And He knew the Laws, mysterious and inviolate, would weave together the weft of mass and energy and the warp of time and space upon the loom of the infinite and the infinitesimal, creating a tapestry of order—a new creation.

And it was so. And God beheld. And He knew the supremacy of the Laws, their consequence. And He was aware of the universe—its awe and its splendor. And God gloried in the cosmos, that which it was and that which it might become. And He sensed that the underlying turbulence fashioned by chaos would, in the cradle of time, alter Nature's creation. And He foresaw the everlasting evolution of the universe and believed it good.

And time now passed. And God cast His eyes upon the heavens. And He saw planets and stars, nebulae and quasars … born out of chaos, dying unto chaos, young and old, and His soul was filled with profound joy. But His joy was tempered by an abiding sadness. For no other was aware of Nature's creation—no other shared His joy.

And He contemplated the wondrous universe. And He saw a multitude of stars and orbiting planets. And one, a mere dust mote among the multitude of planets, attracted Him—a tiny, pale-blue dot—a fragile, blue world. A world that was unformed and void. And in the light of His knowledge was born an extraordinary illuminating idea stimulating His intellect, His inquisitive soul.

And God swept over the tiny blue world and called it earth. Gentle winds caressed its beautiful, blue waters. The nearest star cradled the earth in the warmth of its enfolding beams. And He was pleased by earth and found it good. And God sensed the energy of chaos at the core of the earth. And He knew earth's great potential and great peril. And He knew earth to be a special place, its potential as a light amongst lights unto the universe.

And God spoke but was not heard. "Let the light of this world be a dazzling luminescence unto the universe for good and well-being." And God saw the light brought illumination and understanding. And He knew it was good. And he called the light reason. And its brilliance was intense and unbalanced. And God was concerned. And in His wisdom, He wedded light with darkness in balanced harmony. And the darkness He called faith, for it was unseen. And reason, He proclaimed the master of faith in all that was knowable. And He pronounced that faith must be subservient to and empower reason—that the reason for faith is to have faith in reason. For God was with reason, and reason was God, and the elegance of His universe was a fount of reason—a challenge stimulating reason. And faith, He proclaimed, must be harmonious and resonant with knowledge. And these were the rudiments of the concordance of rationality and faith and a first day.

And God said, but was not heard, "Let the universe I have created be an expanse above the water, so that its beauty will enhance this world." And it was so. God called the expanse sky. And this he did the second day.

And God said, but was not heard, "Let the underlying chaos, the core of this world, be thrust up, fractal layer upon fractal layer, gathering unto the strange attraction of nature's hand, forming the nascent dry land and confining the waters to the plotting spaces between." And it was so. And there was a great upheaval bringing forth dry land. And God called the dry land earth, and the gathering of waters He called seas.

Life

nd God was pleased. For it was a season of wonder, a time to be born, a time of new life, a season of marvel, and a time of vitality. Upon the seas, He saw flowing within its waters, the sowing of the flourishing elements of life. And the sea and the sun, chemistry and energy uniting in symbiosis, season following season, eon upon eon, the genesis of the complex molecules of the unfertilized ova of the primordial soup. And the warm caress of the sun and the salty, sweet bosom of the sea were His delight. And looking upon the sea, He saw her rapturous beauty. And She was fertile. And He was aroused by her rhythmic waves. And He was drawn to the furrow between the crests of her swelling surges. And aroused, He lowered Himself down unto Her. And His sperm burst forth upon the waters, flooding Nature's womb, seeking Her ova. And solemnly, He observed the waters that carried His seeds, and the wind that carried His seeds, and the clouds that formed from His seeds, and with joy, He wept. And He contemplated, *all the organic beings that shall ever live on this earth shall develop from these primordial life—forms brought forth this day.*

Morning came and God was with Himself, and He sowed His seed. And in the evening, He did not withhold His hand. He did not know which would live, which would prosper, which would die, either this or that or whether either alike would be good or would be bad. And His seeds, cast unto the fruitful earth, filled him with hope that they might sprout...so the earth might reap a harvest from the seeds so abundantly endowed with the alphabet soup of life...the Animating Creation of the Transcendent Genome (ACTG).

And God, lost in the calm of afterglow, thought, *I have shared in the creation of life.* And He dreamed that He had experienced a seminal event of creation within creation. And His life—force, full of prolific diversity and vitality, which He had cast upon the waters, joined with the fertile sea. And there, within, was the womb of life. And He was satisfied this third day.

On the fourth day, God observed with great anticipation, saying, but not being heard, "This day I shall not toil, for life shall be as it shall be." And the sea labored forth, giving birth to life. And the streaming sinews of life swimming with the branching currents flowed into abundant diversity...while others swimming against the currents foundered into dead-end eddies, whirlpools of oblivion, the graveyard of natural selection. And God marveled at the sprouting vegetation filling the seas and growing unto the land, converting carbon dioxide into oxygen. And God saw this was good. And there was evening, and there was morning and a fourth day.

And God said, but was not heard, "This day I will again only observe." And God saw His seed bring forth a marvelous profusion of swarming, living creatures within the sea, upon the land, and in the expanses of the sky. He saw great and small sea creatures of every kind the waters brought forth in swarms and all the winged birds of every kind. And in the triplet, the trinity of life, was encoded the father, the son, the mother, the daughter, and the holy rules of all living things. And innumerable species, genera, and families of organic beings with which the world would be populated descended from common parents, being modified in the course of time. And God, in wonder and fascination, saw new organisms in their embryonic development, recapitulating the development of antecedent organisms—extant or extinct. And the Earth was fertile. And creature upon creature and plant upon plant wrote their history upon the stone of the earth, a tablet of wonders. And God, sedentary, observed and wrote this sedimentary record, this alluvial chronicle, engraving it, fossilizing it, in stone, calling it the "Rock of Ages." And God saw it was good, this fifth day.

Atom

And God said, but was not heard and was not known; "With immense joy ... with eager expectation ... with great wonder ... I dream of magnificent new living things that evolution shall bring forth on this day." And unto His delight countless new creatures were propagated upon the earth. And as the day dwindled into dusk with stardust spawning ablaze in the heavens, there, to God's amazement, stood before Him the most wondrous creature of all ... a creature in His own image. And God did not know. And God stared as if at a mirrored reflection and wept. For now He knew the creature that would share His spirit and His creation and know its wonder. And He called the creature Man. And He enfolded Man within His embrace and breathed His spirit, the light and the dark, reason and faith, intellect and emotions, into man. But God was not aware of the turmoil and chaos that these implanted into Man. And God looked upon Man and saw awareness in the depths of Man's eyes. And He knew joy in the awakening of Man's soul.

And God said, "Let Knowledge and Faith grow in Man becoming the wisdom of My spirit, after My example, so that Man may know, enjoy and care for all of My creation." And God blessed Man and His words were heard, resounding in Man's soul, and He was known. And God saw all that His seed had made and all that had evolved, and found it good. And Man saw all that He had made and all that had evolved. And Man was aware of creation. And there was evening and there was morning, the sixth day.

And the hand of God, upon the heaven and the earth, was finished, and it was the seventh day. And God blessed this day and declared it holy, setting it apart for Man to contemplate the goodness of creation and to act for its benefit, to be stewards of the earth and of the sea, of creatures of the land, and of the water, and of the air; and of mankind. Such is the story of heaven and earth when they were created and evolved.

And God again observed His creation, especially Man. And He spoke to Man saying; "The glory of your evolution is an exaltation of creation and kindling for my soul. Now I shall give thee a name by which you shall be remembered by all the generations of mankind. You shall be known as Atom, for you are unique and the ultimate foundation of mankind." And Atom was pleased.

Eat'n

ow the Lord God knew Atom's need … his need for sustenance and shelter. Therefore the Lord God planted a garden, calling it Eat'n, a sign of his love for Atom. And therein grew every plant and tree that was pleasing to the eye and good for sustenance. Within the midst of the garden, He planted the Tree of Life and The Tree of the Knowledge of Good and Evil. And the Lord God took Atom settling him in the Garden of Eat'n, to till it and tend it and to be nourished by it. And the Lord God commanded Atom saying, "Of every tree of the garden you are free to eat; but as for the Tree of the Knowledge of Good and Evil, you must not eat of it; for as certainly as you eat of it, you shall cause a scourge upon the future of mankind."

Lo, the Lord God looked unto Atom. And Atom tilled and tended the Garden. And He was pleased. And He appreciated in Atom an inborn nature compelled to seek knowledge. And in Atom's tender care, by his intellect and growing knowledge, the garden was fertile, increasingly lush and beautiful. And God saw Atom's joy in this and was glad. But He also discerned a deep and downhearted loneliness in Atom's spirit. And the Lord God understood, thinking; "It is not fitting for Atom to be alone, companionless; he needs to share his thoughts and his feelings, as I so needed, and to know the joy of doing good deeds unto another, to love and share. Yea, I shall make for him an equal."

Woman

nd God took a seed from Atom's body and united it with His own seed and breathed into it His spirit. And in this manner He brought forth another Man and She named her woman. And God saw that woman was in Her image. And God gazed upon Her as if looking upon a mirrored reflection and wept. And Atom looked on in wonder and said, "Thank you Lord for this woman ... seed of my seed, and seed of Your seed and of Your spirit; and I shall love and cherish her." And God replied, "As I have so done, you will so do. Woman and man shall join their seeds for pleasure and in love, for this shall be a joy onto life. And from their union will they know the sweetness of life and the joy of Our creation." And as God spoke, Atom and woman were tightly entwined in their nakedness. And God saw it was good. And Man shared His wonder.

And the two, Atom and woman, were naked, embraced in love and full of desire. Without inhibition, while in Her eye, they gently and sweetly caressed, knowing the beauty of their bodies created by God. And God saw their caresses and kisses and knew another of the wonders of Her creation. And their tumescent creation arose His spirit. And as their lovemaking reached climax, God wrapped Her arms gently about them and sweetly breathed the wonder of life and His creation deeply into their souls, and they knew blissful joy and peace. And God said, "Blessed art thou man and woman for I have given unto thee great joy and pleasure in making love. In thy joy shall thee renew thy spirit ... and in the bliss of shared intimacy will be found our creation."

God watched. The Garden gave them sustenance. Its beauty and mystery sparked their desire to understand their world. And they sought Knowledge. And their search enhanced their awe in the wonders of God's creation, reaffirming their Faith. And in the darkness of the night, awestruck by the firmaments, their passion for knowledge was overpowering. And the darker the darkness the greater didst the firmaments glow, all speckled with stars and streaked with flowing gossamer "milk." Lying on the soft warm earth gazing upward at the heavens, they wondered about the making and pondered the workings of the celestial spheres, of the starry, starry night. And the magnificence of the heavens inspired their Faith that Reason would lead to comprehension of creation. Their passion for knowledge was thus cradled by creation. And their sanctuary was harmonious Knowledge and Faith. And God was pleased, for day and night, light and dark, knowledge and faith were in balance; each compelled by and in harmony with the other. And God knew that knowledge and faith were in the nature of Atom and woman. And He was delighted.

And God watched them in their nakedness, man and woman, beloved by Him and onto each other. But their joy was incomplete. For the seed of intellect planted in the fecund loam of their soul grew mightily. And they thirsted for greater knowledge.

The Tree and A Snake

And day merged into night … sunrise into sunset … full moon unto full moon … years unto years. Each moment divinely perfect, each the same. The garden was heaven providing completely for the sustenance of their bodies. But limited was the sustenance for their growing intellect. Listlessly they wandered the tedious and monotonous paths of the Garden, and they were devoured by ennui. And their aimless wanderings on His plotted pathways intentionally always led to the tree … for all paths, all roads, no matter where they might roam, led to the tree and its centrality in the garden … central in their lives … forbidden … provocative … enticing.

Seeing the Tree, they often questioned one another, "Why didst He say unto us: 'You shall not eat of the Tree of Knowledge—Knowledge of Good and Evil?' Without the Knowledge born by this Tree how may we tell good from evil? Can righteous conduct, ethical deeds or honorable actions be chosen in ignorance of good and evil?"

And they desired to know His purpose in placing this temptation before them.

And the force of their intellectual curiosity was multiplied by the frustration of the lengthy time contemplating this unanswered question and they were seized by a powerful impulse launching an inexorable momentum, propelling them to embrace the tree. And while under its towering providence, bright red luscious apples fell upon each of their upturned heads.

And with gravitas they reasoned, reassuring themselves, saying, "Are not all actions of equivalent merit … are not deeds and judgments

14

baseless in merit unless made by knowledgeable choice? Does He truly desire us to live callously in apathetic ignorance? Or does He desire us to act of free will—free will derived from truthful knowledge? To find value in our deeds He must know that they cannot be predetermined or based in ignorance nor constrained by external authority." And they concluded that He had challenged them to act courageously based on their free-will … even if in disobedience.

And they looked up anew and were entranced by the magnificence of the Tree, glimpsing its forbidden fruits, golden and red ripe apples glistening in the morning dew surrounded by dense white and pink blossoms.

A serpent guarded the Tree. They dared draw near … overcoming their fear. And they said unto the serpent, "We have come and desire to eat of the Tree of Knowledge of Good and Evil."

And the venomous serpentine viper tightly embracing the tree, hissed, "The Lord God hasss commanded that you should not eat of this Tree. But do not fear Him, for the Tree isss not God's dominion, but the dominion of Man."

And through glistening fangs, the fork-tongued serpent in sibilant sermon did hiss:

"Ssssave know thisss … once having sssavored of thisss tree, you will sssset in motion that which will remain in motion for the sssweet nectar of the sssuculent fruit borne by this Tree will unleash dilemmas of conscience … of moral introspection. And moreover Truth will no longer be imprisoned by faith … for faith will no longer be the ultimate guide to truth. Rather by doubt, not faith, will you be led to "enquire, and by enquiry … perceive the Truth." Thou may not be of sssufficient maturity to cope with thisss knowledge, itsss moral and intellectual hazards. Eating of this Tree will confound knowledge and faith, emotion and desire, superstition and reason causing conflict in thy soul. Your legsss may not bear thee along the path … nor carry thee through the deepest recesses of your soul … nor sssupport thy wallowing among the deep dark crevassesss of Evil in the World and the reality of the indifference of Nature. Yea, thou shall walk as toddlers on legsss wobbly and unsure through the Valley of Evil and the Unknown. Alas, they may falter and waste away. And thou may ssslither, as I, in the mire."

They heard, but they did not hear. And only the Tree, lush, bountiful with fragrant fruit ripe for eating, a delight to the eye, tempting, filled their senses. And they were eager for Knowledge. And they could not stay their desire. And they ate.

Revelation

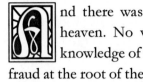nd there was no revelation. No epiphany. No vision of heaven. No vision of hell. No knowledge of right. No knowledge of wrong. And they realized the hoax, the divine fraud at the root of the tree. For the knowledge of good and evil was not within the dominion of the tree, but their inborn attribute, their intrinsic being. Then why this trickery … why this cunning … they wondered? Why? Why the elaborate contrivance?

And they thought. And they searched within. And their eyes were opened realizing that Good and Evil are a human estate and that for God with His unbounded power, His omnipotence and immortality, good and evil were irrelevant. Since He cannot be harmed, so it is that He cannot truly understand good and evil. He cannot truly suffer like man. That He had controlled them, bound them to Him, by authoritarian faith. And so they knew that the true tree must take root in the fertile soil of their own conscience, their own intelligence. That it, The Tree of the Knowledge of Good and Evil, must blossom in the human soul, that good and evil do not exist except in the thoughts and actions of men.

And as they contemplated, the fruits of the tree were transformed. Of the fruit that had been succulent and wholesome, only a portion remained so. Many now grew fetid and full of rot. And as this sight filled their eyes, no longer blinded by His repressive protection, their thoughts were filled with turmoil. And they were alarmed by the chaos wrought in their souls for it was uncontrolled. And they knew the inherent conflict of good and evil. And they were confounded. And they were fearful. And in the conundrum of their nascent knowledge of good and evil, of emotion and desire, of chaos and order … clinging to one another … they experienced the paralyzing uncertainty in each other's souls.

And they heard the Lord God calling in the garden. And creeping and cringing, they approached, groveling in the mire, full of shame. For in knowledge of good and evil, of right and wrong, they discerned conscience and accountability. And they were alarmed by its obligations. And they knew their transgression, their disobedience, in His dominion. And they were overwhelmed. And the Lord God called out, "Where are you?"

And they cared not to hear; calling out, "We do not hear you!"

And God again called, " Where are you? I do not Hear you either. Where are you?"

And they replied, "You do not know!? … Nor do we know … for we are lost in the turmoil filling our souls."

Then God asked, "Turmoil? This is not thy nature, as I created thee." And then God gasped, "You hast eaten of the fruit of the forbidden Tree!"

And Atom confessed, "Our compulsion for knowledge didst overwhelm us. We have … eaten of the Tree."

Then the Lord God said, in anger, unto them, "Because thee ate of the Tree about which I commanded thee, all the days of your lives and all the days of the lives of your progeny, for generation unto generation, good and evil will struggle in the souls and actions of mankind bringing chaos into their lives."

And Atom and woman, as one, responded, "You deceived us, so we have learned from the fruit we have eaten. No longer are we children, in need of your fatherly protection, or your authoritarian control. We thought we knew nothing of good and evil because we thought only the Tree could provide this knowledge. But now we know as the serpent forewarned that good and evil do not exist in the Tree but are inherent in the world and that within us are the innate nascent buds of morality. For we know, since we have eaten of the tree, that our eyes are open and we, who are of your image and your spirit, know that understanding of good and evil, right and wrong, will blossom in our souls. Only by climbing the branches of the Tree of Life by our own volition, out on limbs perilously suspended above the surrounding mire below, can we truly embrace the joys and sorrows all the days of our lives."

Evolve

nd God foresaw that the emotional and intellectual conflict now present within Man's soul would change mankind, generation after generation. And God understood Man's fate and named woman Evolve, because she was the mother of evolving mankind. And God looked upon them with sadness and hope for He knew what must be. And He knew that He could not dam the mighty waters of freedom rolling down as a great torrent, great cataract carrying His children to their destiny.

And God, distant, watched his children. And in Atom's and Evolve's distress, the Garden was ignored, no longer fertile, no longer producing abundance. And it sprouted thorns and thistles. Only by great toil, and by the laborious sweat of their brows, could they produce but meager food. The Garden of Eat'n was blighted by their uncertainty and was fallow.

Now Atom and Evolve knew each other, conceiving a child. And Evolve bore the child, a baby boy. And he came into the world cooing out of joy. And the Lord heard the joyful sounds of the newborn infant. And Evolve and Atom beheld a tiny being in their image, in His image, made of their love. They were overwhelmed and they wept. And the Lord, hearing their joyful weeping and the joyous cooing of the infant, came and was awed by the wonder and beauty of the baby. And there were tears upon God's eyes and joy within Her soul. And God's anger at their disobedience was allayed and She said, "The wonder of your lovemaking, the wonder of your child, you shall proclaim unto all mankind who will issue forth from you. The sounds of newborn infants will always be a call of wonder heralding this blessing onto mankind. And in making love is proclaimed the Original Blessing that I have given unto you. And the pleasures of lovemaking shall always merge Our souls. And the birth of each child ... each born of purity and beauty ... will sanctify mankind and will be My rebirth. These shall always be an affirmation of our creation, and a joy onto all mankind."

And making love was natural and unreserved unto Atom and Evolve. And of this gift from God, did they joyously often partake. And it was a gift of great pleasure and solace given by each unto the other. And they didst know the caress of God. And upon occasion, a child was conceived, a joy from joy. And Evolve bore many offspring, for she and Atom were fertile. The first child they named Bane. A second they named Able, for he would be able.

Bane and Able

ow Bane, first born, was raised in ignorance. Poorly did Atom and Evolve parent unto Bane. Lost in the tempest within their souls was the ability to understand Bane's nature. Neither had they prior example, nor prior experience in caring for a child. Nor could they teach knowledge of right and wrong for they were as toddlers learning to walk the paths of newly found knowledge.

And it came to pass, in spite of the love they bore for their child that their ignorance in his nurturing nurtured the ignorant portion within Bane's nature. And Bane grew to be an ignorant man—a man full of chaos, bearing many of the Tree's evil fruits.

Now Atom and Evolve knew Bane, knowing their errors. And the bane that had been wrought by eating from the Tree, they knew. And they called unto the Lord, accusingly, saying, "We have suffered. And so too, has our innocent child. Help us, for we didst that which we were compelled by thee to do. We forgive thee for thou didst not know what thou didst unto us."

And the Lord answered, "Lo, it is good that we can see in our children how we have erred. So be it. What is done will be undone, slowly, generation by generation. Look unto the light and the dark, Knowledge and Faith, for there are guides that I have placed in your brain and heart. But beware of the perfidy of Faith, for if it conflicts with Knowledge, it will lead us astray."

And they raised Able, knowing their experience with Bane and remembering that which God had said. And Able, nurtured by love and knowledge, was a pride unto his parents.

Now Able became an able provider and he prospered. Bane tilled the soil but was unfruitful. And chaos simmered within Bane and he was distressed. And the ignorance and chaos within Bane's soul begot jealousy, which begot hate, which begot rage. And in rage, Bane set upon his brother Able and killed him within the shadow of the Tree of Knowledge of Good and Evil.

And the Lord came and said onto Bane, "Where is your brother, Able?"

And he said, "You do not know? Am I my brother's keeper?"

Then He knew and said, "What have you done? Hark, your brother's blood cries out to Me. A terrible evil you have committed!"

"Evil?" responded Bane, "I know not evil and I know not good for I am ignorant of these. My parents in their ignorance, in their confusion, in their lack of understanding, could not by example or instruction provide me this knowledge. Neither could they furnish the discipline nor the empathic sensitivity to act honorably." And God was aghast and dismayed. Anger welled up in Him. And as God, in passion, was about to strike Bane, He noticed Able's blood in pools about the gnarled roots of the Tree of Knowledge of Good and Evil, nourishing it, transfiguring its blossoms from white to red.

And God contemplated this metamorphosis. And He said, "I planted this tree and it has become a root of evil. Why did I do so?" And God, introspective, appreciated that He had desired to test Man— to put before Man choices to be made by his free will. And God thought, *but was not my test unjust because of the compulsions I inspired into Atom and Evolve? Was I not a poor parent, authoritarian, failing to teach and to act with understanding and loving tenderness? Did this not predetermine the outcome?* And God understood his complicity, and in compassion, tempered his punishment of Bane.

And God said unto Bane, "When the fault is bared, who must bear the fault? I too must be punished, as you must, for we share guilt. You will be an outcast, a wanderer on Earth, shunned by your brothers and sisters. And your name and the deed it recalls will be the bane of Bane. And to hearken unto the memory of mankind this vile deed, instead of joyful cooing during birth, infants will wail, decrying paradise lost—lost by your deeds. And an infant's cry, a child's cry shall be a compelling empathic entreaty, an encouraging challenge, to be a sensitive, thoughtful, comforting, and wise parent. And I, too, will be an outcast, an exile from Earth, so that Man may evolve freely without my machinations." And He acknowledged unto Bane that in the course of human and divine events, it may become necessary to dissolve the bonds which have connected one with another, and to assume among the powers of the earth and heaven, the separate and equal station to which the laws of nature and of God's nature entitle them, a decent respect to the needs of both require and impel them to be separated. And the Lord withdrew from the presence of Bane and from the Earth, Exile from exile.

Noah Alters God

nd the line of Atom and Evolve was fruitful, becoming numerous on Earth. Now God was withdrawn from Earth during many generations of mankind. And after many years, it came to pass that the Lord was overwhelmed by his inquisitiveness and could no longer resist His desire to return to Earth. Returning, He perceived that the life span of the children of man and woman had diminished. The Lord said, " My breath, giver of long life, can not abide in mankind forever, since they are flesh; let their days potentially be one hundred and twenty years, which they may attain someday by their incentive to obtain Knowledge." Man cannot be God; neither God, man. And in benevolence He withdrew from the infancy of man and the beauty of the earth.

And again God returned. And in his way, by God's unchanged nature, He perceived that the wickedness of pubescent mankind was now great on the earth. And He judged that every imagination of their thoughts and every desire of their heart were only evil. And they didst not have the values that He valued. But Man cannot be God; neither can God be Man.

And self-righteously He wanted them to be, as He desired them to be or not to be at all. And He was a flood ... with rage. And irrationally, He cravenly wanted their destruction and the destruction of all living things that He had made. And the Lord said, "I will destroy man for their values are amiss as I see them. All mankind whom I have created from the face of the earth I will destroy; both man, and beast, and creeping things, and fowls of the air; for I will act without pity and I shall come thereafter unto heaven."

And torrential tears of rage issued from His eyes. And they fell, a great deluge upon the earth.

And so He brought a great flood of tears, of water, of rage. And sweet blue waters, the sweet blue seas, were filled with the salt of His tears. And God had brought forth a great calamity, a great terror. And the seas rose. And all the earth was inundated, ravaged. And dry land was lost from the face of the earth. And drowned were innocent children and innocent pregnant women and innocent beasts. Bloated, they floated upon the water, the sea of His tears, the Holy Sea. And God saw the carnage He had wrought and wondered.

And He looked upon the foul flotsam of death upon the waters and saw a small sanctuary, a small island amidst the lachrymose slaughter. And it was refuge to a small band of survivors. Animals, two by two, encircled a small group of people, all grasping at life. And a noble man, proud and monumental, stood at their center. And the man held in protective embrace an orb, an ark.

And God was drawn to the ark for its power was great. And He looked upon the man and knew Noah. And God said unto Noah, "What do you embrace?" And Noah spoke, trembling, with rage unto the Lord, "An ark … precious unto me. Within is the accumulated knowledge of ethics and concepts of justice gained at great human sacrifice. By unexpected chance, by mutated memes both good and bad, by random change to the twists and bonds of evolving society, mankind has intuitively and reasonably selected moral codes most beneficial for individuals in their communal intercourse. Codes meant for the good of creation … the creation that you now destroy. You who art all-powerful have betrayed our creation. You have placed cruelty before compassion. You have wrought desolation rather than taught morals. Is it not within your power to change the hearts of men rather than destroy them?" Can Man be God; and God be man? And He knew His own baseness. And God closed His eyes ending tears of rage. Many were saved … after many had perished. And He swore an oath unto God assuring that never again shall an "act of God" bring destruction or carnage unto mankind.

And God knew the truth of Noah's words. And He realized that the Tree He had placed in the Garden had provoked mankind's self-determined search for right and wrong—to illuminate the moral way in conflicts of knowledge and ignorance, justice and injustice, chaos and order. And God also knew the friction of chaos and order, ignorance and knowledge within His own soul. And God knowing Noah's virtuousness blessed him and his progeny with a covenant, saying unto them, "Be fruitful and multiply, and fill the earth with honor and good deeds. And unto your stewardship I give my creation. Care for and preserve every beast of the Earth, every fowl of the air, all that lives upon the land and all the fishes of the seas: into the hands of Man are they delivered for their protection."

And God said unto Noah, "I now establish My covenant with you and your offspring to come, and with every living thing. I covenant to never again endanger mankind nor the other creatures of the Earth, while the minds and hearts of Man desire to fulfill the promise represented by your ark—the ark of our covenant."

And Noah built an altar there. And the altar was sanctified by their mutual pledge to be faithful unto their covenant. And God made a sign unto the heavens to confirm the covenant, saying, "My celestial bow will adorn the sky set against a backdrop of rain clouds. Always will it be a sign of our covenant. Behold its exquisite hues, for they symbolize the beauty of diversity. And behold … their unification, illuminating white light, a reflection of the power of Knowledge—the keystone of the arch locking together the ark of mankind's existence and My greatest gifts. When My bow is in the sky, all who see it shall remember our everlasting covenant."

Babel Babble

ow, Noah's descendants were numerous, covering the Earth. And all the Earth had the same language and the same words. And Men migrated to the land of Shinar and settled there. They said to one another, "Come let us make bricks and burn them to hardness." The brick serving as stone. Bitumen as mortar. And they said, " Come, let us build us a city, and two towers with their tops in the clouds. They shall be a monument to our knowledge, ingenuity and industriousness." And a colossal beautiful city with mighty towers, ivory towers reaching the heavens acclaiming their intellectual prowess, arose from the land. The work was arduous. Their creation was celestial. And their satisfaction in their creation was as high and broad as the greatest soaring mountains or as wide and deep as the bluest seas of God's creation. And they were smug about their creation. And they were vain. And the sound and the fury of their conceit reached the ears of God. The Lord drew near. And He was shocked and awed by their creation. And He saw in this creation the promise of his "children" foretold by Noah's Ark. And He knew their growing knowledge and intelligence, self-sufficiency and assiduous nature. And despite the beauty of their creation, He was disturbed.

He bristled at their temerity. And He was jealous, wanting to preserve His hegemony in creation. In order to counter their growing scientific knowledge, advance in reasoning and technological prowess, He sowed the seeds of ignorance and superstition. And He called it religion. In so doing, His egomania was satiated.

And so it was that religion was upon the earth. And God said, "Let there be Darkness and in Darkness shall they worship me." And so it was. And they feared Him and would no longer defy Him. And there was division and decay. And Dark Ages were upon them.

And the Lord confounded their speech. And their speech was Babel unto each other. And parents could neither speak unto their children, nor child unto parent, nor friend unto friend, nor leader unto follower. And they knew frustration. And they knew isolation. And their discourse was no more. And the people in their bewilderment and by the hand of God were dispersed from there, over the face of all the Earth, according to their new tongues. And alas they went ... to babble on. And the Lord grieved. And His heart was heavy ... for He knew the jumble of His creation ... the disjoining of his children ... His creation of a Diaspora of mankind.

Abram

And mankind divided and dispersed over the face of the Earth, was fertile rising up populous nations and cultivating nascent cultures. And in this diversity was beauty. Amongst one of these nations was the man, Terra, who took his son Abram, his grandson Lot, the nephew of Abram, and his barren daughter-in-law Sarai, the wife of Abram, and went forth with them from Ur of the Chaldeans to go into the land of Canaan. But when they came as far as Haran, they settled there.

Now Abram could not be still in that place for the sense of discovery was upon him, a commanding quest to go forth from his father's house to find elusive truth, a promised land. And Abram went forth, he, and his wife, and his servants, and all that he had, and Lot with him. And it came to pass, during the many years of his wanderings, that Abram became a wealthy man earning power by his wisdom and strength, by his kindness and generosity of spirit. But despite his accomplishments, Abram was downhearted. After a time the word of God came upon Abram in a vision. "Despair not, Abram, I am an inspiration unto you. Your bounty is great."

And Abram said, "O Lord, with great gratitude I receive Thy bounty. But wouldst I joyously exchange these blessings for but one gift—the blessing of a child by my wife, Sarai. Unto thee I petition that it be so. For this, we grieve to the depths of our souls." And it was night, full of stars, full of wonder, and the Lord said, "Look upon the heavens and count the stars, if you are able to count them." And He added, "So shall be your offspring." And because Abram put his trust in the light and dark of His spirit, the Knowledge and the Faith inspired by the breath of God, he reckoned to His merit.

And Abram gave thanks unto the Lord. And as the sun set a deep sleep fell upon Abram, and a great dark dread descended upon him sprouting from the roots of the Tree planted deep within his being. And he foresaw his offspring, strangers in strange lands, enslaved and oppressed. In his prescient dream, he knew visions of good and evil … of virtue and vice. In this vision didst he take warning. And from this vision didst he know the exigency of creating a universal code of human ethics. And he knew that the mighty arm of the Lord would not save them but could only guide them. And he foresaw that his offspring would be many and that they would be students of moral principles and teachers of ethics complementing and enriching the community of mankind. And he knew that he would be a great teacher and live to a ripe old age.

And when Abram was ninety years old and nine, the Lord appeared to him, and said unto him, "Walk with Me, side by side, for we are of one spirit." And so they walked together, united.

And God said unto him, "Thy vision is an evolution of the covenant of the ark of Noah; this is the vision, in humility, that I have come to want for thee and for mankind. Thou knowst the obligations we share and because of this I have come in reaffirmation and as custodian of the covenant made with Noah to renew it unto thee. Thee and Sarai shall be the parents of a nation. And thou shall no longer be called Abram, but thy name shall be Abraham for thou shall be the father of multitudes. And Sarai shall be known as Sarah. I will make your line exceedingly fertile, and make a nation of thee. This, my covenant between us, and thy offspring, is an everlasting promise—a promise that I will be a teacher unto thee and unto thy offspring. And a nation of teachers unto mankind will come forth from thee. And this covenant I will share with all mankind so that nations shall be teachers unto nations and they shall not be complacent to ignorance any more."

And God said to Abraham, "As for your wife Sarah, I will bless her; indeed, I will give her a son by thee. I will bless her so that she shall give rise to nations; teachers and doers of good deeds unto mankind will issue forth from her." And Abraham thought unto himself, *can a child be conceived to a man a hundred years old … can Sarah bear a child at ninety.* And God heard Abraham's thoughts and said, " Nevertheless, Sarah will bear thee a son for by my medical intervention shall she be fertile and by my care shall she deliver a healthy child, and he will be called Iact." And God was then gone from Abraham.

Sodom and Gomorrah

pon the plains of Memory, three strangers appeared unto Abraham as he sat in the door of his tent during the heat of the day. Abraham lifted up his eyes and looked, and saw them standing near. Greeting them warmly, bowing, he bid to them, saying, "My lords, if it pleases you, do not go on past your servant. Let water be brought to refresh yourselves and to bathe your feet. Please recline under the cool shade of this tree while we bring you bread." And they replied, "Please, do as you have said." And it was done.

After they were refreshed, Abraham questioned wherefore they go. And they responded, "The outrage of Sodom and Gomorrah is so great, and their sin so grave that the Lord has sent us. For their transgressions, they shall be destroyed."

And Abraham remembered his dream and said, "From where dost their wickedness bubble forth? A corrupt malevolent fountainhead or a clear sweet spring contaminated by its course through adulteration? From innocent blood spilled unto the soil of the Tree conceived with questionable merit? Might not a teacher purify the water or prune the corrupt fruit of the Tree? Surely, He desires not unjust punishment—punishment without compassion ... punishment that would sweep away the innocent along with the guilty? Shall the Judge judge unjustly?"

And they answered, "If we dost find in Sodom fifty innocent ones, we will speak of this onto the Lord."

And Abraham spoke, saying, "Again, I must venture to speak. If the number is but one innocent, should that life be taken, depreciated as collateral damage, while destroying the others? And if men, in

33

ignorance, have committed acts of wickedness but alas have, in knowledge, done deeds of kindness, unto each what measure should be accorded? Is death deserved unto all? Should not the attempt be made to teach them right, in order to weigh the balance to good, as so bound by God's covenant?"

And they answered, "We will consider that which you question when we judge the people of Sodom and Gomorrah. But their destruction is likely, inevitable, for they do not properly act nor believe." And they turned their backs on Abraham. And down onto the plains of Sodom and Gomorrah seeking the two towers of these cities didst they fly with destruction in their hearts ... for they knew the Truth. And down onto the valley of the shadow of death didst they fly to bring shock and awe ... terror and destruction.

And Abraham returned unto his place, heavy of heart.

Lot

And they came to Sodom at evening; and Lot, Abraham's nephew, sat at the gate of Sodom: and Lot seeing them rose up to meet them saying, "Please, my lords, turn aside to your servant's house to spend the night, and therein bathe your feet; then you may be on your way early." And they said, "No, we will spend the night in the square." But he dissuaded them for it would endanger them being in that place, so they turned his way and entered his house. He prepared a feast for them and baked bread, and they ate.

And as they lay down, people of the city, knowing of the strangers, gathered about, girdling the house. And they called unto Lot, and said unto him, "Bring out unto us the men who came in to thee this night, for we desire them. If you do not abide our demands, we shall prevail by violence" And Lot went out at his door unto them. And he said unto them, "These men are my guests and I shall protect them under the shadow of my roof. I beg you, brethren, do not commit a violent wicked deed. Look unto my two daughters who have not known a man. Let me bring them out to you, and you may do to them as you please, but do not do anything to the strangers sheltered under my roof."

And so hearing Lot, his guests, dumbfounded, cried out to Lot, "Thou wouldst sacrifice your daughters to protect us! To deliver them over to evil men, to hurl them into the hands of the wicked is sacrilege. Iniquitous are they who would force another into an intimate act. Rape is an abominable sin. For thee and all must know: 'Do not suffer on to others that which others would not suffer onto themselves.' Let all know that guided by empathy one sets the gentlest course through the crosscurrents of human interaction. Embrace this precept that is more precious than gold—a golden rule which should govern the conduct of mankind."

Now those gathered before the gate did hear this petition. And many knew the truth of the words so spoken. But some who did hear did not hear at all. Nor did some care to understand. And these few continued to press hard against Lot's door, moving forward to break it. But those, whose conscience had heard, truly heard the righteous words, with the might of their outstretched arms, pulled their companions from Lot's door, protecting Lot's family and his guests.

And the strangers were aware of the actions of Lot and the men of Sodom. And they discerned the dichotomy of man's spirit. And they glimpsed the wickedness and they appreciated the goodness of individual men ... the conflict of order and chaos, of knowledge and ignorance in the nature of men. Realizing the truth Abraham had spoken and remembering the words of Noah, in their understanding compassion filled their hearts. And they comprehended that wickedness stemming from ignorance might be transformed with love and the teaching of knowledge. And they pondered their mission. And God was aware. And He pondered also.

Apocalypse

nd a sickly glow filled the predawn sky alighting unto every eye. Gathering doom-filled brimstone-clouds shrouded the infernal raging sun. Sunbeam fingers, yellow-rayed, penetrated the clouds with ghastly light, radiating down unto the plain, casting sinister shadows and terrifying monstrous forms, bringing fear to every door.

And then suddenly a big bang thundered, reverberating across the plain … a terrifying drone of impending destruction flying over the plain … a cataclysm ferociously shaking the world. A tempest burst forth with fire and brimstone pouring down from the heavens. And a flash of brilliant blinding light radiated across the plain, a star alighting on the earth … and then … ascending to the heavens … an enormous nightmarish mushroom cloud.

And the strangers spoke out, passionately, "Oh, say … you can see by the dawn's early light … the power of Nature, God's discovered might." And the strangers were heard.

For harm was neither wrought unto Sodom and Gomorrah nor upon the gathered trembling terrified people. And the people cried in fear and relief for they were saved from the apocalypse that He could have wrought unto them.

And the strangers said, "The Lord has not taken your lives nor destroyed your cities. For some have acted honorably. And others were innocent of evil. Learn well the power of the lessons taught this day."

And the mushroom cloud dissipated, revealing the mountain which it had encircled. The mountain no longer a perfect cone was transformed into the shape of a mushroom, sculpted by God. And engraved upon the granite surface of the mountain was a beautiful bas-relief portraying the wonders of creation. And in the relief were hand and footholds. And the people climbed up onto the mountain, unto the history of creation, their joy mushrooming by seeing and touching the poignant rendition of creation … casting ajar the Gates of Paradise. And there upon they observed the escape of God from the ark and the beginning of creation. And they were drawn to the narrative of the big bang, learning of the power God had acquired in breaking the bonds of the ark. And they cried, for they were thankful that so powerful a weapon had not been used to destroy them. Elegantly engraved thereon was the story of Atom, the power of the bonds in his Nature, illustrating the wonder and horror in their breaking, in the unleashing of those bonds. And the tears falling from their cheeks dropped as rain unto the mountain. And rivulets flowed downward from the apex to the nadir of mankind's earthly existence. And the salt of their tears gathered upon the relief, unto creation, like snow upon the mountain. And so it was that His anger bowed to His compassion.

And Abraham stood at the place where he had spoken with the strangers. And he looked down towards Sodom and Gomorrah, unto anticipated new Pains of Memory. And he didst see to his astonishment the cities intact—the towers still standing. And incredulously, a freakish mountain resembling a mushroom covered with salt, the salt of tears. And with a wry grin he knew his wisdom had prevailed. And Abraham had great hope.

And the mountain, God named Sodom Ha'lide … to remember the SALT of joyous human tears and Abraham's passionate and courageous entreaty for diplomacy and forbearance averting utter devastation … mass destruction. And so it was and so it will be remembered on the Plains of Memory.

Iact

nd now the Lord visited Sarah. And the Lord harvested a seed from Abraham and a stem cell from Sarah. And He didst a wondrous thing—joining their fertile cells together enveloping them with his spirit and in His code. So didst He conceive an embryo, placing the growing and dividing cells in Sarah's nurturing womb. And Sarah bore them a son in their old age. And Sarah and Abraham saw their baby in their own image and were overwhelmed with joy and they wept at this miracle. And Abraham, as commanded, named him Iact; for they knew he would grow into a man of action, doing good deeds. And the child grew and was weaned. And Abraham made a great feast on the day that Iact was weaned. And many of his household saw there the son of Hagar, Ishmael, and made sport of him for he was not born of commitment and love but out of exigency, from a concubine, and they drove him away. And when known to Abraham, this thing was a very grievous injustice in his eyes. And in frustration, he spoke onto his household and God also heard, "A child, no matter the circumstances of its conception, is one of the most beautiful of God's blessings onto mankind. It is contemptible to condemn a child because of its parentage. My love for Ishmael is equal to my love for Iact. I cherish them both and neither is greater nor lesser in my heart." And God heard the voice of Abraham and said onto him and his household, "Of both Ishmael and Iact will I make great nations, for as Abraham has spoken, so is the truth."

Sacrifice

nd thereafter, it came to pass that the Lord did test Abraham saying unto him, "Take now thy son, Iact, whom thou lovest, and get thee into the land of Moriah, upon one of the mountains of which I will tell thee."

And Abraham rose early in the morning, and saddled his ass, and took two of his young men with him and Iact, his son. And they rose up, and went unto the place where God led them.

And God spoke unto him, saying. "Now ye shall gather wood for a burnt offering." And it was done. And the wood was arranged upon a rocky sacrificial altar.

And Iact said, "Behold the wood and the rock, father, but where is the lamb for the burnt-offering?"

And the thunderous voice of God spoke unto Abraham, commanding, "Prepare thy son, Iact, for thee shall sacrifice him unto Me!"

And Iact cried out in terror unto Abraham his father, "My father!"

And he answered: "Here I am, my son."

And Abraham wept and looked unto his son. And Abraham knew. And Abraham called unto God answering, "NO! This I will not do. I will not sacrifice my child, or any living being, for that which you command is evil and unconscionable. I defy Thee! I will not obey. I will not commit such a loathsome act. You should know that which is in my heart without testing me thusly! Who are you? I know not! I despair of your virtue. The God who would be teacher unto my children and my children's children must be merciful and loving, recognizing that all living beings are to be treasured. Compassion and wisdom must be His essence. He would not ask this of me, to sacrifice my blood, my child, graven in His image. No! God would not need such an abhorrent test to know my faithfulness. Do unto me that which you must but do not harm my child."

And God answered, "Your defiance is the righteous answer I sought. For lo, it is, unto Me, anathema that a father would sacrifice his son. This must never be! Thou shall not sacrifice, nor martyr, nor scapegoat, any living being to prove faithfulness or to absolve sin. This law you and all mankind shall abide by forever. Your courage and wisdom are a rock of life, a validation of my laws and a foundation for mankind. You are not only graven in My image but your soul has been filled with the best of My breath—inspired with compassion and love."

And Abraham lifted up his eyes, and looked, and beheld before him a ram caught in a thicket, caught by its horns: and Abraham went and took the ram, and freed it from the thicket and released it—a symbol of his compassion. And lo, he beheld laying at his foot a horn from the ram, cleaved by its struggle. And Abraham took it as an offering. And placing it unto his lips, he trumpeted a resounding song of joy—calling unto God and men, a reminder, to "show far" and wide, in space and time, this revelation, this epiphany, founded in "compassion and love."

And again the Lord called down from heaven onto Abraham, and said; "I bless you because of your courage and your wisdom, for your understanding of the beauty of life. I will bestow My blessing upon you and make your descendants as numerous as the stars of heaven and the sands on the seashore. And they will go forth, a beacon for knowledge onto mankind."

And such was the binding of God by Abraham. As well as the binding of father to son ... son to father.

Rebecca

nd Abraham rose up and he and his household went together to Be'er-she'ba and dwelt there. And they prospered.

And Sarah's lifetime was a hundred and twenty-seven years. And Sarah died in Hebron. And Abraham mourned and wept for her. And in mutual kindness and respect, Abraham negotiated with Ephron for the cave of Machpelah. And Abraham therein purchased the field and the cave and the cave became the burying-place and tomb of Sarah.

And Abraham was old and Iact his son was unwed. And Abraham said unto his son, "Before my death I pray that you shall take a wife. Go unto my country, unto my kindred, and there take a wife. And Iact said unto his father, "Father, I desire to do as you request for I am ready to take a wife. I hope to find amongst your kindred the woman whom I shall love and who shall love me and whose wisdom and integrity shall be my joy and an honor unto our people."

And Abraham looked upon his son and said, "I have known you to act wisely in all I have set before you. Please, my son, follow your head and your heart to find true love. As you wish, so I hope it will be. And do not do so solely to gratify an old man's designs." And Iact took ten camels with his father's blessing and departed; having goodly things given by his father as gifts, and he arose and went unto the city of Nahor.

And Iact was uncertain. He did not know how he would know but know he must. Upon entering the city, Iact made the camels to kneel down by the well of water at the time of evening when women came to draw water for their flocks. And Iact said, "O Lord, the God of my father Abraham, send me good speed this day, and show kindness unto my father." And Iact moved the stone off the mouth of the well and gave water unto the camels and bade the flocks to drink, attending their needs. And so didst he ignore his own extreme thirst. And he considered unto his heart and unto his mind how he would know the woman who might become his wife. And as he went to quench his thirst a young damsel, very fair to look upon, with a pitcher on her shoulder, came up to him. And she said onto him, "Drink, my lord, sate your thirst. Your lips are parched by lack of water. It honors me to serve you. I have seen the kindness of your soul, for you provided for your animals before you attended your own needs." And she hastened, and let down her pitcher upon her hands, and gave him drink. And Iact looked steadfastly upon her, knowing unto his heart and soul the sweetness of the water flowing into her cupped hands from whence he drank.

And Iact knew. And he asked of her, "Whose daughter are you? Tell me, I pray. And is there a man who holds your heart?" And she answered, "I am Rebecca, the daughter of Laban, the son of Milcah, whom she bore unto Nahor, the brother of Abraham." She said moreover, "My heart is mine alone. Within is a chamber for another to dwell." And he said, "Blessed be the God of my father Abraham, who has led me safely to the land of my brethren and where I hope I may dwell in your heart." Then Jacob kissed Rachel and told her that he was her father's kinsman, Abraham's son. And the damsel brought him to her house knowing him in her heart, and told her mother's house according to their words. And it came to pass that Iact asked Rebecca to be his wife and he resided in her heart. And he said onto her family, "I wish Rebecca to be my wife with your blessing for I cherish her. And I desire her to return with me unto my father's abode." And they called Rebecca, and said unto her, "Will you be this man's wife and go wither he may go?" And she said, "I will go in love." And they blessed Rebecca and Iact, saying unto them, "Be thou parents of thousands, of ten thousands, and let thy seed inherit the gentle ways of Rebecca. And so may they open, through kindness, the gates of those who would consider ill unto them." And Rebecca arose, and her damsels and they rode their camels, and followed Iact. And Iact brought her and her servants unto his people, unto his way.

Return

nd when they had journeyed reaching the land of his birth, Iact took Rebecca and went out to meditate in a field at the eventide; and he lifted up his eyes unto her, and saw and beheld her. And he knew he was blessed. And they walked in the field, knowing their love would sow a rich harvest.

And Iact brought Rebecca unto his mother Sarah's tent, and they took each other, and she became his wife. And he was beloved unto her and she beloved unto him, and they cherished each other. And Iact was comforted for his mother and Rebecca for her family. And Abraham knew their joy.

And Abraham gave gifts of his knowledge, of his spirit and of his wealth unto Iact and Rebecca. Gifts to fulfill their destiny as he foresaw. And unto his remaining progeny he gave gifts of his soul and his property so that they might go into the world with assurance. And these are the days of the years of Abraham's life, which he lived, a hundred threescore and fifteen years. And Abraham expired and died in a good age, an old age, an old man and full of years, full of kindness, good deeds and love. And he was gathered to his people. And he was gathered unto his loved ones and God beheld. And his children, and his children's children and all of his seed buried him in the cave of Machpelah, in the field of Ephron the son of Zohar the Hittite; the field which Abraham purchased of the children of Heth. There was Abraham buried, and Sarah his wife. And it came to pass after the death of Abraham, that sagacity brought fortune to Iact, his son.

Begetting

nd those who had begot, begot; and those begotten, begot … so it had been, so it was and so it would be. And these were the generations of Iact, Abraham's son: Abraham who begot Iact. And Iact dwelt by Beer-lahai-roi. And Iact was forty years old when he took Rebecca, the daughter of Bethuel the Areamean, to be his wife. And Iact entreated Nature's God for his wife, because she was barren; and He was entreated on Iact's behalf, and Rebecca, his wife, conceived. And the child struggled within her womb, so that she also struggled within herself, saying: "This being, being as it must be, wherefore do I cope?" And she inquired of the Lord. And the Lord said unto her:

> "Two nations clash in thy womb,
> Two separate peoples to harmony shall come
> By thy gentle love and teaching;
> Each people will have virtues and faults;
> And for the common good each will serve the other."

And when her day to be delivered was fulfilled, behold, there were twins born unto her. And the first came forth ruddy all over like a hairy mantle: and they called him Hesaw. And after Hesaw had opened Rebecca's womb, then came forth his brother, his hand holding tightly onto Hesaw's heel; and his name was called Jacob— Hesaw's strength, Jacob's ingenuity in synergy at birth.

And Iact was two score and ten years when Rebecca bore them. And the boys grew. Hesaw was a watchful and skillful hunter, a man of the field; and Jacob was a quiet and thoughtful man, his soul dwelling amongst men. Iact and Rebecca loved Hesaw and Jacob. And Rebecca would soften the hearts of her sons unto each other knowing their character and their differing destinies.

The Birthright

ow Jacob had made pottage; and Hesaw came in from the field, and was faint with hunger. And Hesaw said to Jacob: "Let me swallow, I pray thee, some of this red, red pottage; for I am faint." And Jacob said: "Sell me first thy birthright." And Hesaw said, "Behold, I am near unto death; and what profit shall the birthright be unto me? Gainsay our inheritance would come with obligations and commitments that would constrain my freedom. And would thou not bestow all my rightful benefits unto me?"

And Jacob said, " Yes, my brother, I swear that I would give unto you the deserved entails of our father's estate. So swear unto me first"; and he swore unto him; and he gave his birthright unto Jacob. And Jacob gave Hesaw bread and pottage of lentils; and he did eat and drink and rose up, and went his way. And so it was that Hesaw turned away from the responsibilities of his birthright.

Land Promised

nd there was a famine in the land. And Iact went unto
Abimelach, king of the Philistines unto Gerar. And the Lord
appeared unto Iact, and said: "Go not down into Egypt;
dwell in the land I will tell thee of. Sojourn in this land, and I will
be with thee, and unto thy progeny. I will give all these lands, and I
will establish the oath which I swore unto Abraham thy father; and
I will multiply thy seed as the stars of heaven, and will give unto thy
seed all of these lands; and thy seed shall profit all the nations of
the earth blessing all, because Abraham was an honorable man unto
whose teachings I did hearken.

And Iact dwelt in Gerar. And he was prosperous. And he waxed
great. And he had possessions of flocks, and possessions of herds,
and a great household. And all the wells he dug filled with water. And
the Philistines envied him. And the Philistines contended for the
water saying: "The water is ours." And Iact gave unto them all the
wells they contended. And he removed from the Philistines, and dug
another well; and for that they strove not. And he called the name of
it Rehoboth; and he said: "For now the men hath made room for us
for we have been generous unto our neighbors, and we will be fruitful
in this land." And the Lord appeared unto him that same night, and
said: "I am the God of Abraham thy father. Fear not for I am with
thee. In peace you have benefited your fellow man and for this I will
bless thee, and multiply thy seed."

And Iact built an altar there, and called upon the name of the Lord.
Then Abimelech went to him, and Ahuzzath, his friend, and Phicol
the captain of his host. And Iact said unto them: "Wherefore are
ye come unto me, to once again steal the benefits from my works?"
And they said: "We have plainly benefited from your work and your

kindness, and we say, "Let there now be an oath betwixt us and thee, that we wilt do no hurt unto each other and we wilt work for the common good." And he made them a feast, and they did eat and drink. And they rose up betimes in the morning, and swore one to another; and Iact helped them on their way, and they departed in peace.

And it came to pass the same day, that Iact's servants came and told him concerning a new well, which they were, digging, and said unto him, "We have found water." And he called it Shibah. Moreover, the name of the city is Beersheba unto this day.

Guile

nd it came to pass that when Iact was old, and his eyes were dim, so that he could not see, he called Hesaw his elder son, and said unto him, "My son", and Hesaw said unto him: "Here am I."

And he said, "Behold, I am old. I look upon the day of my death. Now take, I pray thee, thy weapons, thy quiver and thy bow, and go out to the field, and take me some venison; and make me savory meat, such as I love, and bring it to me, that I may eat, that I might bless thee before I die." And Hesaw did as he was bid.

And Rebecca heard that which Iact spoke to Hesaw their son. And Rebecca, knowing the character of her sons, spoke unto Jacob telling that which Iact had spoken unto Hesaw, saying, "Go now to the flock and fetch me from thence two good kids of the goats; and I will make them savory meat for thy father, such as he loveth; and thou shall bring it to thy father, that he may eat, so he may bless you before his death."

And Jacob said to his mother: "This deceit I will not do unto my father. Another iniquitous act I will not do unto my brother."

And Rebecca said unto him, "Your father's blessing must be unto you for it is appropriate to your destiny and would be a burden unto your brother. Your father does not see his sons as they are but as he would have them be. He does not accept that which he saw when Hesaw willingly gave up his birthright. Nor could he accept that which he saw when Hesaw desired to avoid the responsibilities that would encumber its advantages. Though the act by which you gained Hesaw's birthright was improper, he gave it up readily because it was not in his heart to keep it. Thus is it with this blessing. Your father remains bound by tradition and blindly wouldst give the blessing to his first born despite the appropriateness. Now do as I tell thee for I am thy mother."

And Jacob said to Rebecca his mother, "Behold Hesaw my brother is a hairy man, and I am a smooth man. Our father peradventure will feel me, and I will seem to him a mocker and this deception detected will cast a shadow on his soul and I will bring a curse upon me from my own father, and not a blessing."

And his mother said unto him, "If so, upon me be Iact's curse, my son, for truly I make coin of thy loyalty to me. So hearken to my voice, and go do that which I command."

Blessing Bestowed

nd he went and brought them unto his mother. And his mother made savory food, such as his father loved. And Rebecca took the choicest garments of Hesaw, her elder son, and placed them upon Jacob. And she put the skins of the kids of the goats upon Jacob's hands, and upon his smooth neck. And she gave the savory food and the bread, which she had prepared, into the hand of her son Jacob.

And he came unto his father and said, "My father."

And Iact said, " Here am I, who art thou, my son?" And Jacob said unto his father, "I am Hesaw thy first born. I have done according as thou bade me. Arise, I pray thee, sit and eat my venison, that you may bless me."

And Iact said unto his son, "How is it that thou hast found it so quickly, my son?"

And Jacob said, "Because the Lord thy God sent me good speed."

And Iact said unto Jacob, " Come near, I pray thee, that I may feel thee, my son, and know thee."

And Jacob went near unto his father. And his father felt him and said, "The voice is the voice of Jacob, but the hands are the hands of Hesaw." And he discerned him not. And he said, "Bring it near to me, and I will eat." And he did eat. And Jacob brought him wine, and his father drank.

And his father said unto him, "Come near now and kiss me my son." And he came near and kissed him. And he smelled the smell of his raiment, Hesaw's raiment, and blessed him, saying, "See, the smell of my son is the smell of the field, which the Lord hath blessed and mankind is sworn to protect. So God, give thee of the dew of heaven, be a teacher unto those who desire to be taught and seek the teachings of the wise. Serve thee thy people using knowledge. Be an example unto nations lifting them up from ignorance. Be a leader who leads honorably. Show love and compassion for thy people. And be a blessing unto all and so be blessed. And may it be said of you that he saw the soul of his people and in so seeing he saw the path of good deeds and love."

And it came to pass when Iact had made end to the blessing of Jacob, he was weary and fell into a deep repose. And he dreamed of a kid of the goats who spoke with him in Jacob's voice. And he knew he had been deceived. And he was a blaze consuming the deceivers. And the Lord came to him and said, "Iact, douse your fire, doth not burn in rage, for thou hast not dealt honestly with thyself. Thy self-deceit has doubly blinded thee—closing your eyes to the world about thee and the world within thee. Thou knowest the character of your sons. And yet thou accepted the deceit as if a lamb to slaughter. Accept that which thy knowledge sees in thy soul. Now thy children have an uneasy peace. Do not render them asunder. At Babel, by my anger, my children were scattered. In thy anger do not act rashly. Do not scatter thy sons one from the other. Think upon the reasons that caused thee to be so easily fooled." And Iact saw that he had not only been blind of eye but also blind to knowledge, full of self-deception and blind faith, avoiding the truth that he did not wish to see. And Iact thought upon this as he awoke unto the presence of Hesaw. And he knew.

Hesaw

nd Hesaw had also made savory food, and brought it unto his father; and he said unto his father, "Let my father arise, and eat of his son's venison that thy soul may bless me." And Iact his father trembled exceedingly, saying unto him, "I have eaten of savory foods before thou came, believing they were brought by you, and I have given your blessing unto Jacob."

When Hesaw heard the words of his father, he cried a great and bitter cry, and he said unto his father, "Bless me, even me also, O my father."

And Iact said, "Thy brother came with guile, and hath taken away thy blessing."

And Hesaw said, "Is not he rightly named Jacob? For he hath supplanted me these two times taking away my birthright and, behold, now he hath taken away my blessing."

And Iact in understanding and compassion, with love, said unto his son, "Behold, I act on behalf of you and your brother. Deep in my soul I knew I was not bestowing my blessing unto you. Now I understand. I shall teach you and in so doing I shall bless you, for I love you deeply."

And Hesaw lifted up his face unto his father and wept.

And Iact, his father, continued, "Behold, my son, does a rock give forth water? No, for it is not its nature. Is it in Hesaw's nature to be bound by the responsibilities that are inherent in the blessing, which was thine, but given to Jacob? And so be it with thine birthright. Your nature, your fulfillment, requires freedom from these obligations. Your birthright and your blessing would have been a burden unto you. You wouldst live to curse them and me. They are better suited to Jacob's nature."

And Hesaw, he saw also that to which his father had been blinded. And he realized its truth, and he said unto his father, "Hast thou but one blessing, my father? Bless me, even me also, O my father."

And Iact, his father, answered and said unto him, "Behold, of the fat places of the earth shall they be thy dwelling and sanctuary. And of the dew of heaven from above will fall unto you and its sweetness shall always fill your heart with the joy of freedom. And thy mighty arm will be a bulwark serving and protecting thy nation in virtue. And it shall come to pass that you shall be a nation, a nation in brotherhood with other nations."

Jacob's Ladder

nd Hesaw and Jacob were brothers blessed by their father in truth and knowledge, out of love. And Iact sent Jacob away to Padden-aram to take a wife from thence. And Jacob went out from Be'er-she'ba and went toward Haran. And he lighted unto a place, a place full of the beauty of the earth, awe-inspiring. And he could not tarry from there for his spirit was transcendent and he took some of the soft loam of the place and put it under his head, and lay down in that place to dream.

And he dreamed. And he beheld a ladder, endless, set upon the earth, and the top of it, unseen, reaching into the firmament. And upon it he beheld mankind, soul after soul, generation upon generation ascending; climbing tediously, ceaselessly, inexorably upwards one rung followed by another but occasionally, sadly, profoundly, failing and faltering, shattering rungs, falling downward.

> How bright, how dull, how noble, how craven,
>   How bewildering, how glorious, is man!
>   Resolutely climbing from naught to wonder,
>   Challenging the rungs of being's endless ladder!

And Jacob's spirit was drawn to it, mounting rung by rung. And every rung was but a small step for each man … but a giant step for mankind.

And at the beginning, and at the end, was the moral spirit of mankind, leading, following.

And as Jacob climbed, he beheld below him mankind ascending against a backdrop of verdant green treetops, of amber waves of grain, of purple mountain majesties, and of magnificent turquoise oceans and billowy white clouds, and the earth was a beautiful blue marble, and then a blue dot. And above he saw ascending mankind reaching the moon and the sun, planets and stars ... heaven ... creation. And, behold, Nature stood with him upon the ladder, and She said, "I am the sustenance for the body and spirit. But mankind must be my advocate and defender. And they shall be the seed the earth. Spreading east-to-east, west-to-west, and ever the twain shall reap; by tilling wisdom from mysteries of sky, earth and sea, in advancing scientific feats. And the ladder between heaven and earth will be knowledge in learning my secrets and in nurturing loving care. And thee and thy seed and all the families of the earth shall be blessed with my beauty. For I will not leave those who, for better or worse, cherish my nature."

And Jacob awoke from his dream, seeing his world, seeing the progress of mankind stimulated by nature, and he said, "Surely, the Lord is in the beauty of the natural world! These wonders are none other than the elegance of Nature and a golden gate unto heaven."

Leah and Rachel

nd Jacob rose up and went on his way. And he came to the land of the children of the east. And it came to pass that Jacob found his brethren, Laban, his mother's brother, in this land. And Laban said unto Jacob, "Surely, thou art my bone and my flesh." And he abode with him the space of one month. And Laban said unto Jacob, "Because thou art of my family, shouldest thou therefore serve me for naught? Tell me, what shall thy wages be?" And Jacob said, "I will labor for thee for bread upon my plate and shelter against storms. And for thy good council in managing of the land, its crops and animals."

And Laban said, "This is a good thing and I will do this for thee, abide with us." And Jacob served Laban, and years were unto him but only a few days, for all that he learned.

Now Laban had two daughters. Their visage was as one. But the spirit of one was as night ... the other as day. And their sisterhood was the beauty of sunrise and sunset. The elder was Leah. The younger was Rachel.

Leah's eyes didst seek knowledge. Now Leah was of profound intellect and her physical beauty mirrored depth of her intellect. Exploring mysteries of nature were her love. To behold her was to know the essence of reason and the beauty of creation. And desire for knowledge burned forth from her reason kindling the spirit to create math and science out of intellect. She sought a husband who would respect her council. But men were intimidated by her scholarly temperament.

Rachel's eyes were full of mystery. Now Rachel was gentle of spirit and her physical beauty mirrored its sweetness. Unexplainable mysteries of nature were her love. To behold her was to know the essence of the beauty of creation. And artistry burned forth from her virtuosity kindling the spirit to create beauty in the arts out of passionate intercourse with creation. She sought a husband who would share the expanse of her spirituality and the depth of her love.

And Rachel didst find joy in the movements of her body graven in Her image. And God knew her. And the silken threads of Her robes flowed down from the heavens and upon them didst Rachel climb upwards unto Her. And as she didst climb, the silken texture of Her robes brought her joy. And in her joy she did dance unto the sky.

And Jacob saw the beauty of Rachel's spirit. And Jacob loved Rachel. And Rachel loved Jacob. And Jacob admired Leah for her intellect. And by it he was intimidated.

Deceit

nd Jacob asked Laban for Rachel's hand. And Jacob said unto Laban, "I love thy daughter, Rachel, and she loveth me. I have served thee well and well have I been taught by thee. Give Rachel unto me for my wife, for our souls will always be bound to each other's; only together will our days reach fulfillment."

And Laban gathered together all the men and women and children of the place and made a feast. And it came to pass in the evening that Laban brought forth his veiled daughter unto Jacob. And he went forth unto her. And they were wed.

And Jacob upon their wedding bed raised the veil. And it was not Rachel but Leah. And Jacob rose in anger and said unto Leah, "What is this thou hast done unto me? Did I not serve thy family in good faith? Didst I not fulfill my contract laboring seven years for Rachel's hand? Wherefore hast thou beguiled me?"

And Leah said, "My father hath brought me unto thee for I am his first born daughter. My sister may not wed before me. For thus hath we deceived thee. And My father knows that I love thee."

And Jacob in bitter rage cried out, "Laban! What hath thou done unto me by your guile!" And as a rampaging wild river did he rage forth from the wedding tent consummated not by love and joy but by defiling violent rage.

And Laban heard his cry. And he met him with drawn sword. And Jacob said, "Thou hast deceived me."

And Laban said unto him, "By our custom, it is unfitting for a younger daughter to wed before her older sister. This thou should have known."

And Jacob said, "Wouldst thou therefore condone this deceit? Didst I not serve thee for Rachel? It is Rachel that I love. It is she I wish to take as my wife and she desires me. By your treachery, I am not my beloved's and my beloved is not mine. Wherefore art thou my Rachel? Hast thou also beguiled me?"

And Leah following behind Jacob cried out, saying: "It was for my welfare that this has been done by my father. He desires my happiness and knew of my love for thee. I would cherish thy love. But if thou cannot love me …"

And Laban, interrupted, saying: "Jacob! Thee will honor the vows thou hast taken this very day or by my word and by sword my eldest daughter will be a widow on this her wedding night!"

And Leah said, "Father do not harm this man for he is surely my husband by law even if not by spirit. And though he does not love me, I do him. If Jacob agrees to honor our vows, I will accept thou giving my sister, Rachel, unto him as wife also."

And Laban said, "But if this be done in this manner, Jacob must fulfill your week, my daughter Leah. And more, he shall serve me yet another seven years for Rachel's hand."

And Jacob thought upon Leah and Rachel.

And Leah brought Rachel unto them. And he looked unto her with love and she unto him with love. And Jacob lifted his voice unto Rachel and Leah, "Despite your father's treachery, Rachel and I will never find peace if we consummate our love, as it must be, by stealth, doing unto him as he has done unto me. Listen unto me, for I know that for our best, I must accept my marriage to Leah. I will gladly provide for her and be kindly unto her. And, despite the bad faith of our first contract, I will, in good faith, make a new contract unto your father that I may also wed Rachel."

And as he didst so speak, Jacob concealed the seething emotional turmoil in his soul. And while consummating his new commitment with his father-in-law, he silently made another to himself—one-day Laban would garner harm grown of his deceit.

And Laban too agreed. And Jacob fulfilled Leah's week; and then Laban gave unto Jacob his daughter, Rachel, to be his wife.

And Jacob went unto Rachel, and he loved Rachel, and he served Laban yet seven years more.

Parity

And Rachel loved Jacob. And Jacob loved Rachel. But from their love they could not conceive and they were barren. And when Rachel saw she could bare Jacob no children, she was grievously saddened, and she said unto him, "Behold, my sister Leah also loves and desires you, go in unto her." And Jacob went unto her. And the Lord saw that Jacob provided kindly unto Leah, and knew her pain for she didst love Jacob. And He opened her womb. And Leah conceived, and bore Jacob a son, and she called him Reuben for she said, "Because the Lord hath looked upon my affliction, now my husband will love me." And she conceived again, and bore another son, and thought, *Because the Lord hath heard that I am less than Rachel in Jacob's heart, He hath therefore given me another son for I am in His heart.* And she called his name Simeon. And she conceived again and bore a son and said, "Now will my husband be joined unto me because I have borne him three sons." Therefore she named him, Levi, meaning joined unto him. And she conceived again, and bore a fourth son and Jacob was kind unto her but did not love her. And she thought, *I must bear the knowledge of my fate and its burden…in conception is not conceived love.*

And Jacob was heavy of heart for he loved Rachel and desired to conceive a child by her. And guilt weighted greatly upon his soul for his good fortune in having healthy sons by Leah. But Rachel was barren. And Rachel despaired and also knew Jacob's despair. And Rachel pleaded unto the Lord, "God, hath thou given me my misfortune because I gave my sister to my husband?"

And God harkened unto Rachel, "You gave your sister to your husband in love and in consideration of great suffering, for you are kind of heart. For this I would not punish you. Have faith in the beauty of your love and knowledge of the blessings it bestows." And She remembered, and She opened her womb, and she conceived. And she bore a son. And she called his name Joseph.

Justice by Trickery

nd it came to pass, when Rachel had borne Joseph, that Jacob said unto Laban, "Send us away that we may find our own place in my country. My household and I who have served thee and learned from thee, let me and my people go, for thou knowest that I am prepared and ready to venture forth."

And Laban said unto him: "You have found favor in my eyes. I have observed the signs and know I have been blessed on thy behalf. Appoint me thy wages earned, and I will give it."

And Jacob said unto him: "Thou knowest how well I have served thee, and how thy flocks have fared with me. For little thou had when I came, and your fortune has increased abundantly by my care. And now I must make provisions for my own house."

And Laban said, "What shall I give thee?"

And Jacob said, "I shall tell thee tomorrow."

And Jacob took council with Leah and Rachel for he knew the powerful wisdom delivered of the fusion of their character and intelligence. And a clever plot grew out of their cunning. Bold was their scheme, not minutely sheepish. A scheme meant to get Laban's goat, pull the wool over his eyes and butt his butt,. Roguishly off-color, they were certain that the plot's simplicity would assure their success. Neither did they fear being found out nor concerned that they would dye by Laban's hand. And dark was their anger. Their mission not speckled in the least by ruefulness. *Justice be served*, so thought Jacob.

And Jacob returned unto Laban and said; "Thou shall pay me aught, if thou will do this thing for me. I will again pasture thy flock and keep it. And over the remaining years of my servitude, let me pass through all thy flocks, removing from thence every dark one among the sheep and spotted and speckled among the goats, and of such shall be my households' and mine. Such shall be my wages. In the future shall my righteousness witness for me hereafter, when thou shall come to look over my flock, everyone that is not speckled and spotted among the goats, and everyone not dark among the sheep, you shall count as stolen."

And Laban said: "Very well, it shall be according to thy word."

And so as years passed, Jacob removed the sheep and goats according to their contract and gave them into the care of his sons. And his sons set pasture for Jacob's growing flock at three days journey between themselves and Laban's flock shepherded by Jacob.

And as the years passed, Jacob overheard the words of Laban's sons saying, "Jacob has taken away all that was our father's, and of that which was our father's, he hath gotten all his wealth." And Jacob beheld the countenance of Laban and it was not as before. And Jacob was pleased. And Leah also saw the signs in her father's face and counseled Jacob saying: "I see my father's countenance, that it is not kindly toward us as before, he begins to understand our plan—we must leave this place!" And Jacob found her council wise. And Jacob rose up, and set his household upon the camels and he carried away all his flocks, and all his substance, which he had gathered, the flocks of his getting, to return to his land—the land of Canaan.

Confrontation

And it was told unto Laban after the third day that Jacob's household had fled. And he saw the flocks that remained— that they were weak and meager. And anger boiled in his soul. And he took his brethren with him and pursued after them seven days journey and he overtook them in the mountains of Gilead. And Laban came up unto Jacob. And Laban said unto Jacob, "What hast thou done, that thou hast outwitted me, and carried away my wealth and carried away my daughters? It is in the power of my hand and in the will of my soul to do thee great harm."

And Jacob answered and said unto Laban, "Dost thou not know that I didst not realize that I could not escape thee. I travel with my entire household and thou only with men to do battle. Therefore why wouldst I do such a thing? I have deceived thee as thou did deceive me, a deceit for a deceit. And still thou dost not understand the whole of it. And so shall I tell thee, that we may make our peace. The greatness of my flocks has been gained by guile. For we have tricked thee by dyeing each to our advantage. And so I planned, but came to realize the wrong of it. Wherefore I didst flee secretly, knowing the anger that would possess your heart. For lo, I hope that now you understand the outrage of being deceived."

And Laban contemplated this and said, "Thy lesson is well taught. I ask for your forgiveness."

And Jacob said, "And in forgiveness I shall set it right by thee. Now let us walk in peace together among the flocks and divide them fairly."

And so it was done, and their anger was spent. And both had learned knowledge of their heart and the harm they might do. And they made a covenant that they would remember these deeds to their betterment.

Reconciliation

nd early in the morning Laban rose up and kissed his daughters and grandchildren, and blessed them. And Laban departed, and returned unto his place. And Jacob and his household went on their way, to return to his homeland.

And Jacob sent messengers before him to Hesaw, his brother, unto the land of Seir, the field of Edom. And he commanded them, saying, "Thus shall ye say unto my lord, Hesaw: 'Thus says thy servant Jacob. I have sojourned with Laban and stayed for many years. I come with my household, my wives, and my children. May it be that we may be reconciled? And I have oxen and asses and flocks and men-servants and maid servants and I send word unto my lord, that I may find favor in thy sight.'"

And the messengers returned to Jacob, saying "We came to thy brother, Hesaw, and moreover he cometh to meet thee, and four hundred men with him!"

Then Jacob was fearful and full of remorse. For within his conscience were still the rumblings of the perfidious deceits toward his brother. And he was distressed for he did not know his brother's intent. And he divided the people that were with him and the flocks and the herds and the camels, into two camps. And he said, "If Hesaw comes to one camp and smites it, then the camp left shall escape." And Jacob said, "O God of my father Abraham, and the God of my father Iact, O Lord, who said unto me, return unto thy country, and to thy kindred, and do good unto them. I am not worthy. I have bent the truth to my advantage. My staff is no longer strong. It no longer bears its burden. Broken, now I am become two camps." And he lodged there that night and took from that which he had with him livestock for presents to be given unto Hesaw, his brother. And he delivered them into the hands of his servants. And he commanded them, "When Hesaw my brother meets thee, he will say thus, "Who art thou? And whither thou goest? And whose are these before thee? Then thou shalt say, 'They are thy servant Jacob's; they are a present unto you my lord; and behold, he follows behind." And so the gifts went ahead with his servants.

And Jacob left his entourage, lodging that night alone. And he was alone, with himself only. And he could not sleep for he was restless with conflict. He wrestled with a man ... himself. And he fought with the wrenching discord of the docket of his evolving values within his psyche, straining to hallow his mind, fitfully, bit by bit building, advancing his character. *Where is the honorable balance between being "I," my instinctive self-interest ... my freedom to do as I please ... and the responsibilities and limitations of my being "US," my need to be a part of family and community? "IF I am only for ME, who will BE for me, and if I be lost in US, who will I BE?"* And the light of the rising sun cleared the mists of his nightmarish struggle and shone upon the path to follow with comforting clarity. And he saw, he comprehended, that human virtues would prevail if only mankind persevered upon an empathic path wandering through imperfect yet maturing human values, evolving human ethics which might some day be truths held self-evident. He realized that he must act by reason and empathy to discover the noble, the moral principals for human interaction leading to enlightenment. And that the common good would be good in common to himself and the community of mankind if based in wisdom and not chained to dogma. Moral codes, he saw, are real only in the domain of mankind and by codes appointed mankind would be afflicted or nurtured, to the greater loss or the greater good. And he was calm, and no longer did he wrestle with himself. And he said unto himself: "Let me go, for a new day is born." *I have striven with selfishness and unselfishness, the chaos, within my being and have prevailed.* And

Jacob called the name of the place Penance *for I have seen myself face to face, and my soul is preserved.* And the sun rose upon him and the shadow passed from him. And thereafter, the children of Israel were taught not to eat the sinew of pigged self-vanity. And this is taught unto this day because he was touched to hallow his conscience and his reason.

Brothers

And Jacob lifted up his eyes, and looked, and beheld Hesaw, and with him four hundred men. And he ordered in ranks his household with Rachel and Joseph hindmost. And he himself passed over before them, and bowed himself to the ground seven times, until he came near to his brother. And Hesaw ran to meet him, and embraced him, and fell on his neck, and kissed him and they wept.

And Hesaw lifted up his eyes, and saw the women and children, "Who are these with thee?"

And Jacob said, "My household whom I hath gathered unto me by love." Then the household came near and bowed down.

And Hesaw said, "What meanest thou by all the flocks sent ahead unto me?"

And Jacob said, "In the past I hath wrought wrong against you, my brother. This I regret. To bind our kinship in love, to find favor in your sight and to show my sincerity I have sent them as a token of contrition, a gift, unto you."

And Hesaw said, "I have enough; my brother, let that which thou hast be thine."

And Jacob said, "Nay, I pray thee, for now knowing favor in thy sight, this gift unto thee is given freely and not out of regret but out of love. Take, I pray thee, my gift that is brought to thee; because thou hast dealt graciously with me and because I have an abundance." And he urged, and Hesaw took it. And unto each and each other was peace.

And Hesaw said, "Let me now leave that we have found favor." And so Hesaw continued that day on his way to Seir. And Jacob journeyed to a new place, and built a home for his household and made booths for his cattle. Therefore he named the place Succoth, a place of booths. And his household resided there for many years. But in time Jacob and his household left Succoth and came in peace to a new city in to the land of Canaan and encamped before the city. And there he bought a parcel of land where he spread his tent.

Dinah

And Dinah of Jacob's household, his daughter, went out to market and to see the daughters of the land. And Shechem the son of Hamor the Hittite, the prince of the land, seeing her was beguiled and so she with him and he desired her and she him, and they lay together secretly in love. And their souls did embrace one unto the other. And Shechem spoke unto his father Hamor, saying: "Please, I beg thee, arrange that I may wed this damsel for I love her." And Hamor, the father of Shechem, came unto Jacob to petition unto him. Now Jacob had heard rumor and thought his daughter defiled but Jacob held his peace. And the sons of Jacob came in from the field for they had heard of it, and also heard Hamor's petition. Concealing their wrath, desiring revenge to restore their honor and their sister's honor, they were silent but resolutely judged that this thing ought not be done.

And Hamor spoke unto them, "My son, Shechem, loves your daughter. I pray you will give her unto him to be his wife. And make ye marriages with us; give your daughters unto us, and take our daughters unto you. And you shall dwell with us. And we shall conceive a great nation."

And Shechem said unto Jacob and Dinah's brothers, "Let me find favor in your eyes for your daughter has smitten my heart. Whatever you shall say unto me I shall give. Ask me for dowry and gift, and I will give as you request, but please, I beg thee, give me your daughter, your sister, to be my wife."

And the sons of Jacob answered Shechem and Hamor, his father, with deceit, concealing the turbulent waters in the depth of their souls, and said unto them, "We cannot do this thing, to give you our sister to one who is uncircumcised, for that were a reproach unto us. Only on the condition that if you will be as us, that every male of you be circumcised, then we will give our daughters unto you, and we will take your daughters unto us, and will be one people. But if you do not hearken to our words, to be circumcised, we will be gone." And Jacob gave affirmation of the plan proposed.

And their words pleased Hamor and Shechem. And the young man agreed to this thing because he had delight in Jacob's daughter. And he was honored above all of his father's house and now felt he would gain the honor of Jacob's house. And Hamor and Shechem, his son, came to the gate of their city, saying, "These men are peaceable with us, therefore let them dwell in the land, and trade therein, for behold our land is great enough for us all. Let us take their daughters to us for wives, if we should find love among them, and let us give our daughters unto them if they shall find love amongst Jacob's tribe. But, only on this condition will these men agree to dwell with us, to become one people, if every male among us be circumcised, as they are circumcised. Shall not their substance be bound to ours, if so done? Together we shall be a great nation." And unto Hamor and unto Shechem harkened all of their city. And every male was circumcised, all that went in the gate of the city.

And Dinah knew of all that her father and her brothers had asked. And that which Shechem had accepted so they may be forever together. And she knew she must be with him, to nurse him and to love him.

And it came to pass on the third day, when the men of Hamor's kingdom had been circumcised, were in pain and unable to defend themselves, two of the sons of Jacob, Simeon and Levi, brought to each of their brethren their swords. And of this Jacob had no knowledge nor had they related to him their plan. And they came upon the city unawares, and slew all the males. And in their furor,

Simeon and Levi, covered in the blood of their vengeful deed, moved among the corpses, looking for the body of Shechem, for they savagely, mindlessly, desired to despoil the despoiler of their sister. And there among the defiled bodies of those they had slaughtered, they saw the hooded cloak of Shechem. And in their madness, in anticipation of gazing upon the sweetness of revenge, they roughly removed the hood. And in unison their scream reached unto the unfathomable abyss of their souls, merging therein with the evil of Bane placing his mark upon them. For before them, they beheld the dead face of their beloved, avenged sister, Dinah. In death, Dinah silently told her story in loving embrace, her blood flowing freely, joining that of her beloved. And they beheld in her encircling arms the maimed remains of Shecham, her lover. And they knew that she had loved him. And they knew that the perceived transgression was the misconstrued, the seed of their own perverted distortion. And looking upon the body of their beloved sister, they cried out as excruciating grief, a sword, stabbed deep into their hearts. And they were aware that their vengeance was a mobius of vengeance unto themselves.

Infamy

nd Jacob heard their wailing. And he came unto them, seeing all the evil they had done. And saw among those murdered his own cherished daughter, lifeless arms embracing Shecham. And he was overwhelmed with grief and overwrought with pain. And in execration and revulsion for their treachery and desecration, Jacob trembling in anger, said unto Simeon and Levi, "You! You have 'sucketh the honey of her [sweet] breath'. Oh my heart … it shrieks … stung by the venom of your ill-conceived vile sanctimonious act. To be … it is … not to be … for it need not have been. An appalling deed you have perpetrated making you, my own sons, odious unto me. By thy will, driven by your debased craving for revenge, thou hast done a great evil—an evil that will leave the mark of bane upon you unto your death. Here is your sister murdered by her own kin. And next to her the man who loved her—the man she must have also loved. Do you now understand? Is one's honor cleansed by murder? Do you comprehend that she was not taken against her will? Did you smite her in credulous belief that she had besmirched our honor? By murder, you have prostituted honor! Family honor is not found in murder, there is no honor in honor killing!"

And they approached their father, creeping and cringing, groveling in the mire, full of shame. And Jacob was aghast and dismayed. Anger welled up in him. And as Jacob, in passion, was about to strike his sons, he noticed Dinah's blood in pools about his gnarled feet, rooted, fundamentally to the tree—the tree that tempted Atom and Evolve. And in horror, Jacob contemplated this vision. And Jacob shuttered with painful insight, keenly aware, he knew that he had known, in his heart, the intentions of his sons. And Jacob knew his complicity. And he knew his own disgrace and, in self-mortification, the burden of his inaction. And he was unable to reckon the manner of penance—penance that might bring atonement. And from empathic sentience

77

for those martyred arose an epiphany in Jacob's soul. And Jacob knew profoundly the war between good and evil, forgiveness and revenge, compassion and unbridled misguided passion, and in knowledge of these, said unto his sons, "We have gravely sinned. Vengeance has been brought unto vengeance. 'Vengeance is mine,' sayeth Vengeance. And vengeance has burnt our punishment, bitter remorse and shame, into our souls forever. We shall be bound to Dinah and her love all the days of our lives bringing us never-ending pain. In remembering this, our accursed deed, we will honor her by never again permitting vengeance to rule our household. And this may we teach unto all mankind."

And God said unto Jacob, "Arise and go to Beth-el and dwell there for the deeds done here shall not be to your advantage. You shall leave your wealth in this land as meager atonement to the survivors of this land. And your passage to Beth-el will be fraught with trial and tribulations for your crime. And as you see the innocent among your household suffer so will you know the suffering you have brought unto the innocent of this land."

Then Jacob said unto his household, and to all that were there, "Although some consider us victors, we are not. I forbid the taking of spoils. Plunder or pillage shall no man do. We have prevailed by a grievously horrid deed and it condemns us. To gain from this heinous act would be sacrilege. We have murdered and, as we have been taught in the story of Bane, we cannot stay in the land of our transgression. We must not live amongst the surviving loved ones of those we put to a cruel death. We are commanded to give our wealth unto the survivors of our atrocity, for we have destroyed that which is most precious unto them. In this way may we provide aid unto those we have harmed. Now let us rise in our shame and go to Beth-el, as the Lord, our God has commanded. And in the hardships and ordeals of our journey may we come to understand our nature and find means for expiation for our wrongful deeds."

Is-real

nd they journeyed. And as they journeyed, they would climb every mountain, ford every stream and follow every rainbow hoping to find their dream ... a place where their evil scheming was unknown. But known, it was, to all. And they were not trusted. And they were considered pariahs. Everywhere they were shunned. No one took pity on them. Xenophobia was with the peoples they encountered. Nations would provide no succor unto them. No respite ... no sanctuary ... was there unto the household of Jacob, for they were as lepers onto the human race. And they wandered, suffering terribly from privation of food and water, and illness and prostration. And they went unto Is-real knowing now what they had wrought, seeking redemption. And Jacob heard them and again knew his culpability and their sincere desire for atonement. And he said unto them, "A bad deed has brought us low. In good deeds is your atonement." And as they wandered they did deeds of loving kindness secretly along their way. And in these deeds did the hatred of the peoples about them subside and the harshness of their existence ebb.

So Jacob came to Luz, which is in the land of Canaan. And his entire household was with him. And God appeared unto Jacob for He had seen their growth, their evolution, and He said unto Jacob, "Thy name is Is-real; thy name shall not be called anymore Jacob, but Is-real shall be thy name, for as of now, as a household you are a people, a united nation, some day to be amongst united nations, with a unifying creed and the nascent seed blossoming into a communal empathic soul. Your household, your nation, has begun to know that which IS REAL, a ubiquitous truth, a universality, that acts of kindness, that good deeds, are the beauty and glory of our creation." And He called him Is-real, and his household, His nation, IS-REAL.

And God said unto Is-real, "I am God, deemed Almighty. Be fruitful and multiply thy good deeds; be a nation committed to repairing the world; be teachers and scholars dedicated to teaching kindness and tolerance ... critical thinking ... transforming lives with knowledge ... bringing peace, brotherhood and amazing grace to all mankind."

Passing

And God went up from him in the place where He spoke to him. And Is-real set up a tablet in the place where He had spoken with him, a tablet of stone, and he inscribed thereon the lesson he had learned as an offering of knowledge for all that might come unto that place. And Is-real called the name of the place where God spoke with him, Ekor-el. And they traveled from there, and Rachel had hard labor. And it came to pass, when she was in hard labor that the midwife said unto her "Fear not; for this is also a son for thee." And it came to pass, as her soul was departing that she called his name Benjamin. And Rachel died, and was buried there. And Is-real grieved upon her grave. And they journeyed, and spread their tent beyond.

And it came to pass, that Is-real came unto Iact his father where Abraham had sojourned. And Is-real now had twelve sons bringing joy unto Iact, his father. And the days of Iact were numbered a hundred and four score. And Iact expired and was gathered unto his people, old and full of days; and Hesaw and Is-real, his sons, buried him.

And Is-real dwelt in the land of his father's sojourning, in the land of Canaan. And there the generations of Is-real fed their flocks. And Joseph was seventeen. Now Is-real loved Joseph more than any of his children and he made him a coat of many colors. Its beauty was beyond wonder—a coat of dreams. In the brilliant sunlight its hues were infinite, an infinity radiating unto the beauty of creation, overwhelming and awesome to the eye, an apparition reaching beyond the limits of conception. But in the shade, with light wed to darkness, the coat's brilliance was muted and limited in dimension, less awesome and threatening. And the coat embraced Joseph's body and spirit and colored his dreams. And his brethren, seeing the coat, knew their father loved him more than they and they hated him for it and could not speak kindly unto him. And Joseph dreamed dreams and he told them to his brethren; and they hated him yet the more for in his dreams he was their lord and they bowed down to him. And his brethren envied him and thought evil unto him. And they plotted against him. And it came to pass one day when Joseph joined them far afield to herd their flocks that they conspired to slay him, scheming to make it appear that a wild beast had devoured him.

But Reuven remembered Dinah, saying unto them, "Let us not take his life. Shed no blood; cast him into this pit that is in the wilderness so that he may not find his way unto our household, that he may through his wanderings deliver himself from his own vanity and restore himself." And it came to pass, when Joseph was come unto his brethren, that they stripped Joseph of his coat of many colors that was on him. And they took him and cast him into a pit unknown to Joseph, in a land unknown. And the pit was empty, and there was no water. And the sun and the moon and eleven stars were seen by him, but to him, they did not bow down as previously, for he was no longer Joseph of the multi-colored coat. And in fear he cried out. And a caravan of Ishmaelites came from Gilead, with their camels bearing spicery and balm and myrrh, going to carry it down to Egypt, and heard his wale. And they drew Joseph up out of the pit, and they took him to be sold into slavery in the land of Egypt.

And whilst Joseph was being led into bondage, his brethren killed a he-goat, and dipped the coat of many colors in the blood. And they brought it to their father; and said, "This we have found. Know now whether it is thy son Joseph's coat or not." And Is-real knew it, and said, "It is my son's coat; an evil beast has devoured him." And Is-real rent his garments, and put sackcloth upon his loins, and mourned his son many days. And all his sons and all his daughters rose up to comfort him. And Is-real refused to be comforted; and he said, " Nay, but I will go unto my grave mourning my son." And he wept.

Egypt

nd Joseph was sold in Egypt unto Gotiphar, an officer of Pharaoh, the captain of the guard.

And Joseph was a stranger amongst strangers. And he was a stranger in a strange land. And a slave amongst slaves. And he knew his plight. And it was great. And he recounted his desecration at the hands of his brethren and their betrayal. And he could not restrain his grief for it was great. And it overwhelmed him. And he wept.

And love was a void unto him. And in his despair, in his desperation, he cast his eyes into his own soul. And he was dispirited. And in his introspection, he beheld chaos within the ark of his psyche, the ark of his spirit. And its attraction was powerful. And the energy of emotion therein was mighty. And its gravity was great … drawing Joseph.

And irresistibly drawn, Joseph grasped the ark. Anxious, he feared self-revelation. And he wondered if it was good. And he cried, "Let self-knowledge be my innermost universe, my means of embracing my creation." And the humble hand of Joseph closed upon his ark. And unto his spirit was a big bang–a cataclysm. And a tempest burst forth of emotion and contemplation. And he was aware that he, through his ancestors, had eaten of the Tree of Knowledge of Good and Evil—the Good and Evil of his soul. And he knew his creation … His universe. And he picked fruits from the Tree.

And in tasting the fruits he had picked…empathy and sympathy, benevolence and understanding burst forth unto his universe displacing the void. And Joseph knew that his universe was but one of many bounded by each individual soul—souls unbound by their interconnection with the soul of mankind … and the soul of Nature.

And he realized the infinites of infinities. And he desired to weave together emotion and reason on the warp of the spirit gathering them together in an intertwined many-hued fabric...a synergistic whole. And the sword of his spirit was transformed into the ploughshare of his soul. And he knew peace for he knew his oneness with the universe. And he knew his power and that which he might sow and that which he might reap, and knew it would be good.

Interpreter of Dreams

nd time passed. And Joseph, a slave, cast his eyes unto his fellow men. And he saw their dreams. And he knew his own. And he was inspired. And he foresaw his own fulfillment in plowing the fertile dreams of his fellow men. And the ploughshare of his soul was eager unto their aid, upon their behalf. And it was known unto him that a man with a good heart, who does not act unto it, has no heart at all. And it was known unto him that a man with an empathic soul, who does not act unto it, is a man without a soul. And it was known unto him that a man with a wise intellect, who does not use it in beneficence, is not a man in God's image.

And he acted. And he did so in humility and wisdom. And he gained praise from his master. And his master knew Joseph's character. And Joseph found grace in his sight, and he served him well. And Gotiphar made him overseer over his house and over all that he owned. And his house prospered under Joseph's stewardship. And Gotiphar's power grew in Egypt. And by the wisdom of Joseph, Gotiphar's dreams came true. And Gotiphar got far by the trust he had unto Joseph. And he acclaimed Joseph throughout Egypt, and his wisdom was known, even unto Pharaoh.

And it came to pass that Pharaoh's house was ill favored. And Pharaoh's dreams were void and unformed. And he needed council. And he took council with all the wise men of Egypt. And none could make it right. And none could fledge his dreams. Nor make Egypt soar. And Pharaoh was greatly troubled.

And it came to pass that Joseph was remembered unto the Pharaoh. And Pharaoh sent for Joseph, and he was brought hastily. And he came in unto Pharaoh. And Pharaoh said unto Joseph, "I have need of a man who will save my house and give form to my dreams by his wise council. And I believe that it may be thee, that thou canst change our fortune."

And Joseph said, but was not as yet heard, "Let the dreams of Pharaoh be a light unto Egypt and a beacon unto mankind for good and well-being. Tell unto me thy hopes for upon these may we give form to your dreams. And your dreams will be the seed for action. And thus will your house be healed."

And Pharaoh spoke unto Joseph of that which he hath dreamed. And Joseph gave council. And his council was good in the eyes of Pharaoh. And Pharaoh said unto his servants, "Can we find such a man among thee, a man in whom there is such depth of intellect, of wisdom, and a spirit filled by peace?"

And Pharaoh said unto Joseph, "For as much as thee has shown me, for there is none as wise as thee, thou shall be over my house, and according unto thy word shall all my people be ruled." So Pharaoh set Joseph over Egypt.

And Pharaoh took off his ring from his hand and put it upon the hand of Joseph ... a symbol of his power. And Joseph was second in the land of Egypt. And Joseph went out in all the land of Egypt. And Joseph was thirty years old.

Regent

nd Joseph watched over Egypt and there was plenty. And the earth brought forth abundance by his hand. And Joseph set his will against the will of the people. And he made them store a portion of their crops. And these were brought unto the storehouses of Pharaoh against a day of need. And Joseph gathered corn as the sand of the sea until it was unnumbered; for it was without accounting.

And it happened that dearth was upon the land; and the dearth was in all lands. And when all the land of Egypt was famished, the people cried unto Pharaoh for bread. And Pharaoh said unto all the Egyptians, "Go unto Joseph; what he saith to you, do." And the famine was all over the face of the Earth. And Joseph opened the storehouses, and gave unto the Egyptians. And all the countries came into Egypt unto Joseph to buy corn, because the famine was sore in all the earth.

Now Is-real saw that there was corn in Egypt, and Is-real said unto his sons, "Behold I have heard that there is corn in Egypt. Get thee down thither, and buy for us thence; that we may live, and not die."

And Joseph's ten brothers went down to buy corn in Egypt. But Benjamin, Joseph's full brother, Is-real sent not with his brethren, for he said, "Lest peradventure mischief befall him."

And the sons of Is-real came to buy corn among those that came; for the famine was in the land of Canaan. And Joseph was governor over the land. It was he that sold to all the people of the land. And Joseph's brethren came, and bowed down before him with their faces to the earth. And Joseph saw his brethren, and he knew those who had betrayed him, but made himself unknown unto them.

And as he looked upon them, his spirit was being consumed in a conflagration of chaos. And the fuel of vengeance fed the fire within. And he thought, *a life for a life!* And he wandered dismayed and befuddled within his spirit ... seeking. And there within he found the fruits of the Tree and he knew Bane. And in rage, Joseph set upon his brethren, and spoke roughly with them, and said unto them, "Whence come ye?" And they said, "From the land of Canaan to buy food."

And Joseph said unto them, "I know ye are evil men."

And they said unto him, "Nay, my lord, only to buy food have we thy servants come. We are all one man's sons; we are upright men."

And he said unto them, "Nay, I know thee to be evil men. Evil deeds are written in thy souls."

And they said, "We, thy servants, are twelve brethren, the sons of one man in the land of Canaan; and behold the youngest is this day with our father, and one is not."

And in anger, in passion, Joseph said yet again, "Ye are evil men! Hereby ye shall be sold into slavery, ye shall not go forth other than bound in bondage!"

And they said, "We beg thee, do not this deed unto us!"

And Joseph said, "It shall be done now!"

And his brethren cried unto him, "If thou will not spare us please spare our youngest brother and our father from starvation for they are righteous men. Please send unto them corn that they may be saved."

And Joseph had them bound them with chains. And they said one unto the other, in their foreign tongue, "We are verily guilty concerning our brother. This Egyptian has seen into our souls and seen our guilt. And we are justly punished." And they knew not that Joseph understood their words, for the interpreter was no longer between them. And he turned himself about from them, and wept. And he sent them away from him into the prison-houses of Egypt.

And whence they were gone Joseph contemplated their words. And he remembered their concern unto Benjamin and Is-real. And he wondered.

And in wondering, Joseph once again knew the ceaseless pain of their betrayal. And he remembered his coat of many colors … its beauty. And in his thoughtfulness he saw the vanity of it and knew that his actions as a young man, his hubris, his conceit had given birth to their malevolence toward him. And he remembered that Is-real had openly favored him above all his progeny. And he knew his measure of guilt.

Benjamin

nd Joseph decided. And he sent a trusted servant into Canaan unto Benjamin. And the servant found Benjamin and spoke alone unto him, saying, "Your brothers cometh into Egypt and they cometh to great peril. My master knows they are evil men and wouldst sell them into slavery. My master, in his wisdom, desires justice, if these men, are not as he believes he knows. For if they are upright men than he will not harm them."

And Benjamin said unto him, "I am my brothers' keeper and I will verify that they are upright men."

And the servant said, "I have been commanded to bring you unto my master of your own free will. And if he believes your testimony is truthful you will win his favor and win the freedom of your brethren. But hark, if he believes that you lie he will condemn you to the same fate as your brothers. If you cometh to Egypt with me you are not to tell another the reason that you go forth."

And Benjamin went forth into the land of Egypt. And the servant took him unto Joseph.

And Joseph greatly anticipated lifting his eyes unto Benjamin. And when the vision of Benjamin was real before him he saw to his amazement a young man in his own image as it had been. And Joseph stared as if at a mirrored reflection of his youth and wept.

And Benjamin was confused. And he knew not why this Egyptian, a man of power, wept before him. And an uncertain bond drew him. And Benjamin drew nigh unto the Egyptian and gave unto him a silver goblet—a goblet well used by his father and given unto him. And the

Egyptian, hand shaking, holding the goblet close to his heart, said; "Are you not the youngest sibling that thou brethren hath spoken of unto me?" And he continued, "God be gracious unto thee, my brother."

My brother? And Benjamin was confused!

And Joseph's heart yearned unto his brother. "Have you cometh to provide testimony on behalf of your brethren—men whom I know to be evil."

And Benjamin didst speak, saying, "I do not know why it is you think my brothers to be evil men, nor why it is you called me brother. My brothers are not evil men. They have cared for our father with great kindness. And they have been good unto me, providing for my needs and teaching me kindness. They wander our land searching for our brother who was lost many years ago. In this they are somber and committed. They often spill tears as if they were responsible for his tragic loss."

And the Egyptian spoke, "I have knowledge of your brother and I say again they are evil. But I shall listen to thy words and make you pay according to their truth."

And Joseph commanded the steward of his house, saying, "The brothers I have imprisoned—release them. Fill each brother's sack with food, as much as they can carry, and put golden coins in the mouth of each sack. And command them to go, to get thee unto their land, unto their father. And be it known unto them that their youngest brother, Benjamin, will remain and be a slave unto me. And say unto them, this do ye and only if you be of good courage, each and every, and return unto me, unto my justice, and bring with you your father, the creator of evil doers, his household and your households shall I reconsider your brother's fate."

And it was done. And so did the brothers depart.

Reunion

nd when they were gone Joseph could not refrain himself
before all who stood by him, and he cried, "Cause every man
to go out from me save Benjamin." And there stood no other
with them while Joseph made himself known unto Benjamin. And
Joseph said unto Benjamin, "Come near to me, I pray you." And in
fear he came near. And Joseph said, "I am your brother, Joseph, whom
was lost." And he embraced his brother. And he fell upon his brother
Benjamin's neck, and wept; and Benjamin wept upon his neck. And
they wept aloud, and the Egyptians and the house of Pharaoh heard.

And he spoke unto Benjamin, saying, "Be not grieved. Do not fear
any more. I was lost but now I'm found; was blind but now I see. I
have come hither by fate. And by that fate I have had the fortune to
bring a great deliverance, to save the lives of many. I have been made
the lord of all the houses of Pharaoh and ruler over all the land of
Egypt. And you will be well cared for and loved. And soon you, and
I, will be reunited with our father and all our kindred for as you have
spoken I trust our brothers will act with honor."

And the brothers did hasten unto Is-real and they told him all that
had taken place. And they said unto Is-real, "We must make haste
and return to the land of Egypt for Benjamin is in peril." And his
heart fainted, for his concern, their concern.

And Is-real said, "It is our destiny. Benjamin my son is yet alive. We
shall go and save him before I die."

And Is-real and his household took this journey with all that they had.
And Is-real said unto his house, "Fear not to go down into Egypt,
for we go in peace and request only kindness."

And Is-real rose up; and the sons of Is-real carried Is-real their father, and their little ones, and their wives down into Egypt. And they took their cattle, and their goods which they had gotten in the land of Canaan, and came into Egypt, Is-real, and all his seed with him; his daughters, his daughters' daughters, his sons and his sons' sons.

And they came unto Joseph and unto Benjamin. And Is-real saw his son, Joseph, with uncertain recognition for he did not trust his aged eyes. And he trembled. And Is-real said, "It is enough to see my beloved Benjamin but do my eyes deceive me? Is Joseph still alive and before my eyes?"

And Joseph, second only to Pharaoh, weeping, said, "Behold your eyes see for your heart focuses them with loving sight. I am Joseph your son who has loved you dearly all of my life." And their tears joined together, reunited, flowing together, in their embrace. And Is-real's heart was full. And Joseph's heart was full—full of joy and forgiveness—feeling it might burst in his chest. And he knew his brothers were repentant for they had braved his rancor and persecution in hope of saving Benjamin. And he said unto his brethren, "And now be not grieved, nor angry unto yourselves, for I was set upon and sold hither for my own deeds and for my own destiny. Brothers, you have found good heart for taking the risk you have ventured." And Joseph embraced his brothers kissing each. And he wept. "My years have been filled with famine and feast and always with loneliness. And fate set me before you to save us … a great deliverance."

And Joseph went in and told Pharaoh all that had occurred. And Pharaoh welcomed Is-real and his entire household. And Is-real dwelt in the land of Egypt; and they were fruitful, and multiplied exceedingly.

The Second Book of Moses

Exodus

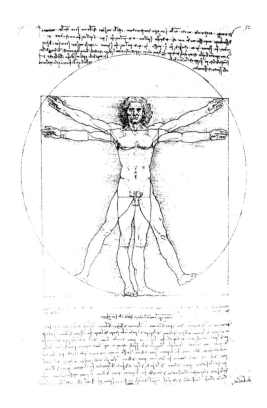

Slaves

ow the children of Is-real, the children of Joseph, were fruitful in the land of Egypt, increasing abundantly and waxed exceedingly mighty so that the land was full of them. And as their good fortune grew, there were new kings over Egypt and they no longer knew Joseph. And one of the kings said, "Behold the people of the children of Is-real are too many and too mighty for us. Come let us deal wisely with them, lest they multiply and challenge our sovereignty in our own land, for should not Egypt be for Egyptians?"

And Pharaoh dreamed of great monuments for Egypt and knew that a great labor force would be needed. Thus they set over the children of Is-real taskmasters to oppress them, bringing them low, making them slaves and burdening them with great affliction. And they built for Pharaoh store-cities and pyramids. And the more the Egyptians gained from the enslavement of the children of Is-real the more the Egyptians demanded of them. And the Egyptians made the children of Is-real to serve with rigor, making their lives bitter with hard work, in mortar and in brick, in all manner of service in the field and in providing for all their needs. Yet despite their servitude, the children of Is-real continued to be fruitful. And Pharaoh decreed that every first-born son born onto the children of Is-real shall be cast into the river.

Now a woman of the house of Levi conceived and bore a son, hiding him for three months so he would not be cast into the river. When she could no longer hide him, she made an ark of bulrushes, daubing it with pitch and put the infant therein and laid the ark upon the river. And the Lord saw the ark and remembered his covenant. Now the daughter of Pharaoh came down to the river to wash herself and saw the ark. And she was inquisitive, sending her maid to fetch it. And when she opened the ark, she saw the child and God filled her heart with compassion. And the daughter of Pharaoh took the babe into her heart and home, providing sanctuary. And she had her maids find the Hebrew who had borne the babe and in secrecy had her suckle the child.

And the child grew up in safety nurtured by Pharaoh's daughter, and he became her son. And she called him Moses because she had drawn him out of the Water. And it came to pass that Moses saw the burdens of the children of Is-real, feeling in his spirit, but not embracing intellectually, that their enslavement was wrong. Now one day he went among the children of Is-real and he saw an Egyptian smiting an Is-raelite. And Moses raised his arm in righteous anger to protect the Is-raelite, striking the Egyptian and smiting him. When the Pharaoh heard of this thing, he sought to have Moses slain. But Moses fled from the face of the Pharaoh, and came to dwell in the land of Midian. And there, Jethro and his family took him in. And he married Jethro's daughter, Zipporah who bore him a son.

And Moses kept the flock of Jethro and his spirit knew the freedom of the wilderness where he shepherded his father-in-law's flock. And the freedom he knew gathered onto his knowledge of the evil of enslavement. And Moses could not find peace, for the knowledge of the plight of the children of Is-real was a burden onto him.

I Am

ow one day as Moses led the flock to the farthest wilderness, he uneasily contemplated the bondage and suffering of the children of Is-real. And he was exceedingly agitated, for he desired to save them, to end the oppression of slavery, but did not know how. And as he followed the flock, he saw a beautiful bush covered in red flame-like flowers—the red of blood, the fire of pain known by slaves abused by the whip—and he knew that he must act.

And Moses said, "I see this wonder and in it I see into myself, that which I must do."

And when God saw his pain and his introspection, He called unto him out of the midst of the bush … "Moses."

And he answered: "Here I am!" And Moses did not know if he heard himself or another.

And God said, " I am God, father and teacher of the children of Is-real, your people."

And Moses was confounded, and spoke unto God saying, "I have seen the affliction of the children of Is-real that are in Egypt. I have heard the cries of their oppression. I keenly know their pain. We must deliver them out of Egypt for their pain is our pain."

And God said, "To facilitate attaining their freedom, I have come. Go onto Pharaoh and say unto him, 'Let my people go.' Bring forth the children of Is-real out of Egypt."

And Moses said onto God, "Who am I, that I should go unto Pharaoh? How will I bring forth the people out of Egypt? If I follow your command … will You go forth with me?"

And God replied onto Moses, "I will guide thee but will not intervene. Only by the flame of your passion will freedom be gained and preserved. This man-made conflict must be settled man to man. You and the Children of Is-real must learn who you are, before you can in freedom be that which you might be."

And Moses said unto God, "Behold, when I come onto the children of Is-real, what shall I say unto them? The God of our fathers has sent me unto you with a great enterprise? And they shall say unto me, "Who is He? What does He expect? Why should I act?" And Moses asked, "What then shall I say unto them?"

And God said unto Moses, "I AM because YOU ARE."

And He continued, "Thus shall you say unto the children of Is-real, 'I AM is the fire of self, the fire of freedom, within thy heart. By this passion, we shall be set free. I AM the spirit in all mankind … I AM is God … I AM is MANKIND."

And God encouraged Moses, "Thus say onto the children of Is-real, 'I AM is a pact made with thy self … it is the power often dormant in each—that power in each person must cry out "I AM" …"I EXIST" … the essential life force in each must be asserted by saying "I AM" … and a nation must know that THEY ARE!" And say onto them, " Declare your independence! All mankind is endowed by I AM with inalienable rights. Do so, so you may live life in liberty pursuing happiness. But it must be remembered that freedom does not come free, for with it come all manner of responsibilities. The man who has the freedom to enslave, is himself enslaved. Freedom, all mankind must know, in knowledge and in action, is an incontrovertible right that must be preserved by the outstretched hand and the mighty arm of all mankind.""

And Moses answered and said: "But they will not believe me, nor hearken unto my voice, for they will say: 'The Lord has not appeared onto you or us.'"

And the Lord spoke onto him, "The message I have given you to bear is compelling and should appeal to their reason and their intellect. Cast the message before them and many will know its truth and accept you and its challenge. For the wonders and the signs that should motivate them must not be tricks of magic nor the force of irrepressible power but their own transcendent understanding of the significance of Freedom."

And Moses said unto the Lord, "Lord, I am not a man of words, neither heretofore, nor since you have spoken unto me, for I am slow of speech, slow of tongue."

And the Lord said unto him, "Injustice has inspired your need to act. Let the flames of your passion consume your insecurity. Do not let the decaying fruits of the Tree of Ignorance fill you with fear and obscure your goal. Now go, use the tools you have … that which life has taught you. Trust in your sensitive intuition, your intellect and have faith in your intuition and your emotions."

Let My People Go

nd Moses went and returned to Jethro his father-in-law, and said unto him, "I must go and return unto my brethren that are enslaved in Egypt." And Jethro said to Moses, "Go in peace."

And Moses took his wife and his sons and he returned to the land of Egypt. And he knew uncertainty and fear.

And Moses returned and he gathered all the elders of the children of Is-real. And bravely he spoke of escape from bondage. And the people learned, understanding and believing in his words; and they wanted to act singing out, "we shall overcome."

And Moses, once a Prince of Egypt, came unto Pharaoh, "Thus say I and the God of Is-real: Let my people go!"

And the Pharaoh said, " Who is your God, that I must hearken unto his voice to let Is-real go? I know him not, for here, am I not The Lord? The Chosen one! Do I not rule here, absolutely? I will not let your people go."

And Moses said, "The God of the Is-raelites has met with me, it is our will that you let the Children of Is-real go! Let us go, lest He fall upon you with pestilence, or the sword."

And Pharaoh was angered. "Dare you threaten me! Go before it is my sword falls upon you. You cause the people to break loose from their work; get you onto your burdens!"

And Moses turned in consternation unto Pharaoh, speaking from the annoyance in his soul. "Thou shall not defy me, for as he has commanded so it shall be. Let my people go, for if you persist in defiance, He will bring terrible acts against thee and thy people. Harken, for these Acts of God will bring down great pain onto your people. Soften the hardness in your heart, before you are brought low."

And in rage Pharaoh spoke, "Acts of your God to be feared? It is my acts that are to be feared! Who speaks in defiance but you? If not raised in my household, I would have your life. Get thee away from me before my heart is truly hardened. Get thee away and thy people to their burdens or suffer death."

Bricks and Straw

nd that day, in anger, Pharaoh commanded his taskmasters saying, " You shall no more give slaves straw to make brick, as heretofore. Let them go and gather straw for themselves. And the count of bricks, which they make heretofore, you shall continue to lie upon them. You shall not diminish ought therefore, for they be idle and plan insurrection, for they cry, saying, let us go."

And Pharaoh's taskmasters went out before the people saying, "Pharaoh has commanded that we cannot give you straw to make bricks. Go yourselves; get you straw where you can find it. And despite this new burden the numbers of bricks you produce shall not be diminished."

And the taskmasters demanded, "Fulfill your works, your daily tasks as when you were with straw."

And the children of Is-real were beaten and demeaned for they could not fulfill their tasks.

And Moses returned onto Pharaoh, saying, "You deal harshly with your servants. There is no straw given to us and yet our taskmasters say unto us, "Make bricks!"; but for the lack of straw we can not make our tally and behold we are beaten cruelly."

Imperiously, Pharaoh responded, saying, "You are idle and in your sloth you dream of things that cannot be, saying you, "Let my people go". Go, now, therefore and work; for there will be no straw given but you shall deliver the required tally of the bricks or continue to be beaten."

And rage enveloped Moses but resolute, he responded bitterly to Pharaoh, "Beware, for the Lord, the God of the Children of Is-real, has commanded that we shall be free. His wrath will be upon you. Plagues He will bring upon Egypt that none can bear and you will, to save yourselves, give us our freedom."

Unimpressed Pharaoh laughed, and said, "You have threatened me before but your God does not act. His power is futile against Egypt and her gods. It is you, Moses, who has brought evil down upon your people by challenging my authority. Go from me. Do not return unto me!"

And Moses left Pharaoh and returned onto God, and said, "Lord, wherefore art Thou? You deal ill with your people! Why did Thou send me onto the Pharaoh? For since I came to Pharaoh to speak in thy name he has dealt ill with your people, neither have you acted in their behalf."

And God said onto Moses, "Why did I send you onto Pharaoh? Do you not know the answer? Does not the intelligence I gave you call out the reason? You hoped, despite my warning, that by My strong hand, by My acts, Pharaoh would let you go. That I, by my hand, would inflict plagues bringing harm unto the guilty as well as the innocent, and that by my cruelty the Children of Is-real would be delivered from cruelty. I have learned from Abraham, from Iact, and from Is-real. It is not countenance of might that I wish to shine unto you but the countenance of compassion and thoughtfulness. And I established my covenant with them, to foster precious wisdom, to teach that the might of reason must master the bellicose power of brawny fight. Freedom will NOT be a gift from me unto thee but an achievement of your mind and your spirit, not of your arm but of your brain and your heart. I have heard the groaning of the Children of Is-real, whom the Egyptians keep in bondage. I remember my covenant. Wherefore I say unto you and the Children of Is-real, you must bring YOURSELVES out from under the burdens of the Egyptians. You must deliver yourselves out of bondage, for your freedom is inalienable but only won and preserved by your own wisdom, your own spiritual strength. You will redeem yourselves with an outreaching mind, with great wisdom and hopefully by non-violent struggle. And in deeds intelligently conceived will you gain your liberty and then I will take you to me for a people, and I will continue to be your teacher, your God. And when you have brought yourselves out of Egypt I will guide you unto the land which I promised to Abraham, to Iact, and to Is-real; and I will give this land unto you as a heritage."

And God again spoke unto Moses and gave him a charge unto the children of Is-real and unto the Pharaoh, king of Egypt, to bring the children of Is-real out of the land of Egypt.

In consternation Moses said, "Behold, I am unable to act because I do not know how to compel Pharaoh to let my people go. Without your help I have been unsuccessful. I do not merit this role. It is a burden beyond my bearing."

And God said unto Moses, " You know the evils of slavery. Tell Pharaoh that he may understand. Make Pharaoh aware of the common good by ending oppression. Now go and know that which is in your mind and in your heart. Present these unto Pharaoh."

Common Good

And Moses was intimidated and confused, a slave to his fear, for he did not know how, alone, he might present his plea. And Moses wandered among his people, knowing the pain in their bondage. And gazing upon the wonder of the mighty Nile, its waters freely flowing, he knew the truth of God's teaching and that he must once more try to convince Pharaoh to "let my people go."

Now Moses again went unto Pharaoh, as God had requested. And Pharaoh was not pleased and his heart was hardened. And Moses said, "Pharaoh, please hear me out. I come to speak of wonders, wonders that will have great meaning and import to you."

And Pharaoh said cynically, "Speak of wonders but be careful of what you speak."

And Moses said, "Please give me audience in the garden where we used to play in our childhood. There I believe we can speak more freely."

And the Pharaoh harkened unto Moses and they passed over from the austere rooms of state to the softness of the evening air in the garden of Pharaoh, a place for gentler discourse.

And Moses brought the Pharaoh's attention to the wonders about them-wonders they had gazed upon as children. The magnificence of the moon and its cycles, the evening star glistening brightly near the horizon and the beauty of the cosmos filling the night. And Moses spoke unto Pharaoh, "Listen and hear the singing of the Nile. Here is a wonder often unappreciated, lost in its prosaic presence in our everyday life. Upon its waters, when but an infant, I was carried to safety from certain death. Your sister's kindness saved my life and set me free, a wonder of human kindness unrecognized. How many other wonders are there—wonders unnoted? The Nile is our sustenance, essential to the greatness of the Egyptian people. You attempt to bend it to your will. But the Nile will not be enslaved. For a time it may indulge you, but when it pleases, it will burst free from its bondage in a furious dangerous torrent. The Nile destroys. The Nile creates. The Nile sets its own course. You subjugate another river, a river of people, a river that has flowed calmly within the banks you have harshly determined. But that river now desires its freedom. No matter whether great stones or tree trunks block its path, the river boils and foams, resistance only will make its fury grow. The river, the children of Is-real, will flood beyond your prescribed banks and become a deluge that will engulf all of Egypt. And your sovereignty will be challenged in your own land. Should not Egypt be for the Egyptians? These are truths. They are not meant as threats for I know that threats will not hold sway."

And Pharaoh, with a hostile heart, said unto Moses, "Speak well for you begin to exasperate me. If you do not convince me now, I will act ruthlessly to insure against insurrection and to maintain subjugation of your people."

And Moses, apprehensive, said in slow deliberation, "Listen, O, Pharaoh, listen to my plea for there are cogent reasons for my supplication. Listen by virtue of the affection your sister has for me. Listen to reasoned arguments, which, once considered, may lead you to great judgments that will be for the good of both of our peoples. And in time will your power grow and the wisdom of the Pharaoh will be recognized onto eternity. Now you question, 'What arguments would draw me to such judgments?' O, Pharaoh, as you enslave my people so are your people enslaved, for he who enslaves is himself enslaved. By the very decrees you have proclaimed, atrocities are brought upon my people. Cruelty begets cruelty. Violence begets violence. Hate begets hate. You and only you have the power to break this cycle unto which we are all held in bondage. By man's very nature he desires freedom. A slave cannot be kept in slavery by kindness. This you well know. To keep slaves in bondage requires force and overwhelming power. And still slaves will be defiant; defiance that must be met with ever increasing brutality. And as brutality increases, desire for revenge increases, continuously escalating, enslaving non-slave and slave."

And the Pharaoh was immersed in thought and looked unto Moses with a softer heart, saying, "Go on."

And Moses continued, saying, "But this is only one argument. The gravity of another you must observe for yourself. Slavery erodes the very sinew that ensures the power of your people. O, Pharaoh, look unto your people for they are becoming utterly dependent unto their slaves who order their lives, infiltrating all aspects of Egyptian existence. Your people have become slothful and apathetic, physically weak from lack of labor, diminished in capability from apathy and scant in initiative. For are there not slaves to labor? Look unto your people and see their idleness. See the cruelty that has become their nature, bred by oppressing their slaves. See how they are but a shadow of their former greatness. And that shadow will spread, dooming Egypt to darkness and corruption of its power. Let my people go! For in so doing you shall let your people go and be their salvation!"

And Pharaoh contemplated these words, and said, "You have spoken with weighty argument. I have to consider your words. Return to me tomorrow as the sun sets."

And Moses left in hopeful anticipation. And the Lord said unto Moses: "Stretch out your thoughts toward heaven, that there may be light over the land of Egypt, the light of wisdom which you have taught." And Moses stretched forth his thoughts toward heaven; and there was a brilliant light in all the land of Egypt. And Moses knew great expectation for the children of Is-real, and for Egypt.

And the next day as the sun was setting and the evening star rose brightly, Moses approached Pharaoh as he had been commanded. And Pharaoh said unto Moses, "Your sagacity is persuasive and powerful while your threats were not. I have gone among my people with new insight and have found truth as you have spoken it. So rise up, get you forth from among my people, and both you and the children of Is-real: go, learn from your Lord, in freedom. Take your flocks and your herds and be gone: and bless us also. May both our nations overcome."

And Moses went to give thanks unto the Lord. And the Lord spoke unto Moses, saying, " You have been an exemplary student using that which I have taught you and your own wisdom to gain emancipation for the children of Is-real. This you have done without harm to your people or the Egyptians—all my people. Speak now to the ears of the people, and let them ask every man of his Egyptian neighbors, and let them ask of every women of her Egyptian neighbors, for any necessities they might proffer freely of their volition for the toil you have endured and for the journey you now face. Also say unto the children of Is-real, each household shall take a lamb and bind it to their door posts so that I may passover each household of the children of Is-real so that they will know my spirit and as a marker so that I can be certain that my flock, the children of Is-real are all gathered to leave this land. The lambs you shall leave as a sign for the Egyptians that the children of Is-real have freed themselves from bondage and will no longer be lead like lambs. But also this will symbolize forgiveness and hope for reconciliation in the future. And this day shall be unto you for a memorial, and you shall keep it as a feast, a memory of the burdens of slavery, so that bondage may be nevermore. Throughout the generations you shall keep it as a feast dedicated to freedom, an observance forever. And for seven days shall you eat unleavened bread so that the memory of the bitterness of bondage will never be put from you." Then Moses called for all the elders of Is-real, and said unto them, "draw out, and take you lambs according to each household, and tie a lamb to your door posts."

And the children of Is-real were urgent in their actions and in haste to leave the land of Egypt. And the people of Is-real did according to the words of Moses. And the people of Is-real made ready to leave. And Pharaoh saw their preparations and came among them speaking unto Moses and the children of Is-real, saying, "We have held you in bondage and have cruelly oppressed you. Now, in peace, we will escort you in safety to freedom … for as I let your people go so do I let my people go."

Red Sea

nd the children of Is-real journeyed, about six hundred thousand on foot. And a mixed multitude went up also with them; and flocks, and herds, even much cattle. And in fear that Pharaoh might have a change of heart, they baked unleavened cakes of dough, which they brought forth out of Egypt, for it was not leavened; because they hastened to leave the land of their enslavement. Now the time that the children of Is-real dwelt in Egypt was four hundred and thirty years. And it came to pass at the end of four hundred and thirty years, even the selfsame day it came to pass, that all the hosts of Is-real went out of the land of Egypt.

And God led the people about, by the way of the wilderness toward the Red Sea. And the Pharaoh questioned their path for they would not be able to cross the sea, saying, " What is this course that we take, we are lead on the wrong path." But Moses said unto him, "We take the path of our Lord. We and you will find a way."

And when the Red Sea drew nigh, the children of Is-real lifted up their eyes, and, behold they saw it was impassable, and they cried out unto the Lord. And they said unto Moses, " Because of this barrier of which the Pharaoh has forewarned shall we be bound to return from this wilderness unto Egypt?"

And Moses said unto the children of Is-real and the Pharaoh, "Fear not, stand still, and see a wondrous sign that the Lord will place before thee recognizing the great judgments of Is-real and Egypt which have brought us to this day." And Moses stepped into the water, lifted up his rod and stretched out his hand over the sea, and it was divided; and the children of Is-real could now go into the midst of the sea on dry land. And all witnessed this miracle and were overcome with wonder. And Moses said, "As the great currents of this sea are split so are the paths of our peoples."

And the children of Is-real went into the midst of the divided sea upon the dry ground; and the waters were walls about them on their right hand and on their left. And the Egyptians watched them as they passed and Pharaoh knew the wisdom of his actions. And as these events passed, God looked upon them, knowing fulfillment and despair. For, as the waters parted, so parted mankind, mankind that He desired to live in harmony. And as the last of the children of Is-real reached freedom, God, in hope and frustration, allowed the waters of the Red Sea to reunite, water on the right hand reaching left, water on the left hand reaching right, embracing. A sign that, some day, all mankind might flow as one.

Stone Tablets

n the third month after the children of Is-real were gone out of the land of Egypt, they came into the wilderness of Sinai. And there they encamped at the foot of a mount. And Moses went up onto God, and the Lord called unto him out of the mountain, saying: "Thus shalt thou say to the house of Is-real, and tell the children of Is-real. Now therefore, if ye will harken unto My voice in deeds, keeping our covenant of loving kindness and gentle teachings, ye and all mankind, who so do, shall be My treasure upon our earth."

And God engraved His words upon a stone tablet for they were of grave import needing to be written in stone. And He gave the tablet to Moses. And Moses bore it, staggering under its weight. And as he descended the mount, his long gray hair flowing behind him; sweat raining from his brow: arms, legs, back aching with his burden, and as he labored he wondered, "Why in stone? Why in stone?" And he continued in a fog of weariness, "Why in stone? Why? Why Almighty this choice? Why this stone to bear your words? Why not a new wondrous device in which to write your words that all might easily carry them at all times? A device to kindle mankind's moral flame, a safe nook in which to contain your commandments!"

And Moses, stumbling down the mountain, came and called all the people and all the people answered together, and said, " All that the Lord hath spoken we will do."

And Moses reported the words of the people unto the Lord. And the Lord said unto Moses: "Lo, I come unto thee to give thee a code of ethics. Go down and bring the children of Is-real before me."

So Moses went down unto the people, and told them and they heard God.

And God spoke all these words, saying: "I am God, who taught thee the value of liberty, so that thee would know the spirit of freedom and free thyself from bondage. Thou shall not accept unto thee irrational faith or any dogma. Of any thing that is of the heaven above, or that is of the earth below, thou shall protect and try to understand; for I, your teacher, visiting inquiry upon thy soul, command that thou use the intelligence I have placed in all mankind.

Please teach and keep My commandments, I request of thee, for we have learned together that these codes bring honor and peace and are to be cherished in our hearts and spirits:

> All humankind are created with equal inalienable rights and thou shall know that each birth is a testament unto the beauty and wonder of creation. Thou shall be committed to liberty, equality and fraternity.
> Thou shall not take thy intelligence that I have given thee in vain; for I, a teacher, will not hold thee guiltless if you do not use reason to understand, enhance and protect our creation and humankind.
>
> - *Remember every day is holy; keep it holy by doing labors that enrich and protect our creation.*
>
> - *Thou shall seek justice by thy reason and compassion; banish vengeance from thy heart.*
>
> - *Thou shall find thy might in thy words and by thy reason, not by the sword.*

- *Thou shall honor all humankind of empathic goodwill, gentle heart and reasoned wisdom and know that elitism, hatred and tyranny are anathema.*

- *Thou shall not kill neither as individuals, as a community, nor as a government unless unavoidably necessary to save endangered innocent life.*

- *Thou shall not steal unless necessary to save a life.*

- *Thou shall not bear false witness.*

- *Thou shall be judged by thy deeds, not by thy thoughts. The thought is not the deed!*

- *Thou shall not rape or molest.*

- *Honor your mother and father if they have been honorable unto you. Parents, honor thy children.*

- *Know not shame if thee covet, for to be covetous is a normal human emotion. Plucketh not out thy covetous eye but see the ethical path by which thy yearning may guide thee to constructive fulfillment.*

The End...The Beginning

And the Shofar blew upon the mount, resounding simultaneously across creation—omnipresent. And the end and the beginning were at hand. And the laws of humankind and the laws of God were one, knowledge of knowledge, faith in faith, and emotion of emotion. And God's Mankind and Mankind's God were heard throughout creation announcing with sound and fury: "Hear, Oh Mankind, We and God are One." God and all of creation are One and Creation and God are One. And creation was everywhere and it was nowhere, a void, complete. And in the void, in heaven, transcendent, were the ordered mass and energy, complementary knowledge and faith, of God, of Man ... of Creation ... within an ark—an orb, a sphere. A sphere ... its surface endless, without boundaries, yet finite ... its geometric dimensions finite and yet bound in its measure to the infinite ... perfect yet imperfect ... imperfect yet perfect ... rational yet irrational ... irrational yet rational ... God and Man ... Creation. And its might ... and its goodness were supreme. And the sphere's gravity was great ... drawing God...

"When I do good, I feel good; when I do bad,
I feel bad, and that is my religion."

Abraham Lincoln

THANK YOU

Thank you for voluntarily reading the second edition of my book. It has been over three thousand years since the first edition was written, literally. My God, I have certainly had a long time to consider how I would approach this new and much-needed second edition! Would you think it would have taken me so very long? Yet, what is a long time for me? I hope in the reading of the new edition of my book you have had a divine and thought-filled experience.

You probably have been startled at my change in attitude. Over millennia, I have been touched, as surely all may be, by the better angels of my nature. Goddamn, over those many years I have come to realize what a pompous, controlling, unforgiving God I am, I yam! Yes, I can use my own name in vain. After all, sticks and stones will not break My bones and names will never hurt me. Well, guess what? I am not perfect nor do I have all the answers. I am not all-powerful! NO, I am not! I make mistakes ... all the time ... bad ones. And there are things I do not know, things I do not understand and things I am emotionally oblivious to. No, I am not almighty! You should notice that I did not provide in either edition some earth-shattering social, scientific or medical revelation ... the way to end wars ... famine ... poverty or a cure for cancer nor the mathematics of the universe. Sorry, sadly I don't have this knowledge to impart. Always had terrible trouble with math and science! Nature does Her own thing. Seems She has a mind of Her own, which I love to rib Her about endlessly. But this

I know, that the stardust of Her Milky Way, is the milk from which we are created. We are stardust stuff.

So hopefully ... "all's well that ends well" ... And in the end, this I yearn, that you, the reader, understand from this book:

Hear, O Reader, You and I are one!

May intellect and reason take mankind out of the wretched shadow of myth and the bleakness of superstition's ...

Midnight darkness dreary,

So man shall never ponder meek and wary

Over a quaint and curious volume

Of ungodly lore ...

nevermore!

Yours humbly ... forevermore,

God

Afterword ...

In the beginning, this poem was the genesis of this book:

And ...
Abraham answered:
No ... I will not sacrifice my
Child ...
For that which you command is
Evil ...
For my Lord ... my God ...
Is merciful and loving
Showing compassion and just wisdom ...
He would not ask this of me ...
To sacrifice my blood ...
My child ... graven in his image

And ...
God answered ...
Your defiance is the righteous answer I seek
Your courage ... a rock of life ...
A foundation for mankind ...
You are not only graven in my
IMAGE ...
But your soul has been filled with my breath ...
Inspired with compassion and love ...

c j stegman

Where's Waldo

Waldos	Page	Source/Inspiration	Credit
"shock and awe"	xiv	Iraq War	Harlan K Ullman/James P Wade
final solution	xiv	Holocaust	
"cruel to make the fault and punish it too"	xvi	Uncle Tom's Cabin	Harriet Beecher Stowe
"the flaming forge of life"	xvii	"The Village Blacksmith"	William Wadsworth Longfellow
"each burning deed and thought"	xvii	"The Village Blacksmith"	William Wadsworth Longfellow
"What is the most powerful force in the …	xix		Albert Einstein
"strong in will … to strive, to seek, to find …	xxi	"Ulysses"	Lord Tennyson
palimpsest	xxii	"Archimedes's Palimpsest"	Archimedespalimpsest.org
"Understand that you are god …	xxiii	Dream of Scipio	Cicero
"Keys to the Kingdom"	xxiv	Matthew 16:19	New Testament
"at the core of religion	xxv	Freethinkers p.52	Susan Jacoby
"begin at the beginning and go on until we …	xxv	Alice in Wonderland	Lewis Carroll
… black … hole	3	Black Hole/no light/ whole universe in ark	
… singularity	3	Gravitational singularity creating black hole	
… shells..	3	Atomic/Egg	
Nil and Bohr	3		Nils Bohr
… something may come from nothing..	3	A Universe From Nothing	Lawrence M Krauss
Blastosphere	4	Early stage of fetal development	
Elegant universe	4	The Elegant Universe	Brain Greene
Pale blue dot	5	Pale Blue Dot	Carl Sagan

Waldos	Page	Source/Inspiration	Credit
Fractal, strange attraction, plotting spaces	6	Terms used in fractal geometry	
Animating Creation of the Transcendent Genome	7	DNA	
Triplet	8	Three base pairs, code for specific amino acid	DNA
... trinity of life ...	8	Holy Trinity	
And innumerable ... course of time.	8	Origin of Species	Charles Darwin
... recapitulating ...	8	ontogeny recapitulates phylogeny	
Sedimentary	8	Sedimentary rock	
"Rock of Ages"	8	Hymn/fossil record	
and God took a seed ...	12	In Vitro Fertilization	
Celestial sphere	13	Ancient Cosmological Model	
All roads, no matter where they might roam	14	All roads lead to Rome (roam)	
in motion will remain in motion	15	Laws of motion	Sir Isaac Newton
Valley of evil	16	"Lord's Prayer"	
days of our lives	19	soap opera ..."Days of Our Lives"	
freedom rolling down as a great torrent ...	20	"I Have a Dream"	Rev. Martin Luther King
Original Blessing	20	Original Sin	
transfiguring its blossoms from white to red	23		Mythology
in the course of human ...	24	"Declaration of Independence"	
to be ... or not to be	25	"Hamlet"	Shakespeare
... Holy Sea	26	Holy See	Pope
... memes ...	26	Cultural "genes"	
... the twists and bonds	26	DNA/RNA	
... sound and fury ...	28	The Sound and the Fury	William Faulkner

Waldos	Page	Source/Inspiration	Credit
... shock and awe ...	28	Iraq war	
... babble on	29	Babylon	
... strangers in strange lands	31	Stranger in a Strange Land	Robert A. Heinlein
... shall not be complacent to ignorance any more.	31	"... and neither shall they learn war any more."	Isaiah 2:4
... collateral damage	33	Collateral damage in war/drone attacks	
... into the valley of the shadow of death ...	34	"Lord's Prayer"	
--a golden rule ...	35	"Golden Rule"	
... outstretched arm..	36	Passover "Haggadah"	
... big bang ...	37	"Big Bang Theory"	
... terrifying drone	37	Drone Warfare	
... fire and brimstone ...	37		
... mushroom cloud	37	Nuclear Weapons	
... by the dawn's early light	37	"Star Spangled Banner"	
... Gates of Paradise	38	Baptistery Bronze Doors, Florence, Italy	Lorenzo Ghiberti
... story of Atom, the power of the bonds ...	38	The Atom ...	
... Sodom Ha'lide	38	Sodium halide/sodium chloride	
SALT	38	Strategic Arms Limitation Treaty	
... mass destruction ...	38	Weapons of mass destruction	
... harvested a seed ...	39	In-vitro Fertilization	
..."show far" ...	41	Shofar ... a Ram's Horn blown in Jewish ritual	
... head and heart	42	"Dialogue Between My Head and My Heart"	Thomas Jefferson
... true love. As you wish ...	42	"The Princess Bride"	
... does a rock give forth water?	54	Moses drawing forth water from a rock	

Waldos	Page	Source/Inspiration	Credit
... a small step ...	56	Apollo 11 moon landing	Neil Armstrong
... amber waves of grain ...	56	"America the Beautiful"	
How bright, how dull	56	"Man"	Dr. E Young
... blue marble ...	57	Earth photo taken from Apollo 17	
... blue dot..	57	Pale Blue Dot	Carl Sagan
... east-to-east, west-to-west ...	57	"The Ballad of East and West"	Rudyard Kipling
... golden gate ...	57	Golden Gate Bridge	
... my beloved's ...	61	"I am my beloved's and my beloved is mine."	Song of Solomon 6:3
Wherefore art thou ...	61	"Romeo and Juliet"	William Shakespeare
... wrenching discord of the docket	70	... he wrenched Jacob's hip at its socket	Genesis 32:25
"If I am only ...	70	If I am only for myself, who will be for me.	Hillel; Ethics of the Fathers 1:14
... truths held self-evident.	70	"We hold these truths to be self-evident ..."	Declaration of Independence
... pigged self-vanity	71	Prohibition against eating pig meat	Kosher Law
... sucketh the honey of her ...	77	"Romeo and Juliet"	William Shakespeare
... to be	77	"Hamlet"	William Shakespeare
Is one's honor cleansed by murder?	77	Honor killings	
Vengeance is mine	78	Romans 12:19	New Testament
climb every mountain ...	79	"Sound of Music"	Rogers and Hammerstein
... amazing grace ...	80	"Amazing Grace"	John Newton
... stranger	83	Stranger in a Strange Land	Robert A Heinlein
... the sword of his spirit ...	84	"... will beat their swords into ploughshares"	Isaiah 2:4
I was lost but now I'm found	92	"Amazing Grace"	John Newton

Waldos	Page	Source/Inspiration	Credit
Declare your independence! All mankind ...	100	"Declaration of Independence"	Thomas Jefferson
... we shall overcome.	102	Civil Rights protest song	African-American hymn
... kindle..	114	Amazon Kindle Tablet	
... safe nook ...	114	Nook Tablet	
... created with ...	115	"Declaration of Independence"	Thomas Jefferson
... liberty, equality ...	115	French National Motto	
... plucketh out the covetous eye ...	116	Matthew 5:29-30	New Testament
"Hear, Oh Mankind ...	117	Shma "Hear! Oh Israel, the Lord our God, the Lord is One."	Jewish Prayer
... touched, as surely ... better angels of (my) nature	119	First Inaugural Address	Abraham Lincoln
... stardust stuff.	120	"Cosmos"	Carl Sagan
"all's well that ends well"	120	"All's Well That Ends Well"	William Shakespeare
Midnight ... dreary ...	120	"The Raven"	Edgar Allan Poe

Biography

he author, Cary Stegman, born during World War II, was fascinated at an early age by science and mathematics. After receiving a Bachelor of Philosophy degree, Cary went on to medical school earning an MD degree from the University of Michigan, followed by a 40-year career as a board-certified Diagnostic Radiologist and Nuclear Medicine physician.

During his years of medical practice, his highly technological specialty underwent an extraordinary "science-fiction-like" evolution spurred by the development of digital imaging modalities. The impact of these incredible imaging advances on healthcare was stunningly awe-inspiring! Extraordinary progress in medical basic science and medical clinical practice was also occurring simultaneously.

To Cary, the elegance of the conceptualization and the brilliant intelligent design of scientists and clinicians bringing their visions to fruition was dramatic evidence of the power of human reasoning and critical thinking. Yet Cary felt the power of critical thinking was often discounted or little recognized in society. Faith and superstition derived from supposedly divine or divinely inspired "holy" text often seemed to inhibit rational analytic thought. Concerned about the potential negative impact of bad social policies based on superstitious dogma, Cary considered how he might elucidate this barrier to wise practices. Reminded of his youthful antipathy to biblical stories, armed with his humanities background and encouraged by discussion with family and friends, he began to write his book...The New Old Testament.

Acknowledgements

hank you to family, friends and acquaintances that have made both great and small contributions to my book. Whether it was by discussion or debate about basic concepts, by sharing their discomfort with biblical stories or religious dogma, by relating personal reactions to passages read in my book or by providing help in editing: all have been a source of encouragement and direction.

Comments were surprising as well as gratifying, ranging from, "I could not continue reading your manuscript because it was too challenging to my basic beliefs making me think too much" to "I could not put it down. LOVED IT, LOVED IT." So many of the comments made my heart beat faster and my fingers move more swiftly on the keyboard.

To the special people who have my heartfelt gratitude and deepest mindful appreciation:

> To my wife, Shirley, who is my Leah and Rachel. Who has found me well, kept me well, loved me well. With whom I have drunk the sweetest of water and with whom I have swam in the saltiest of seas.

> To my mother, Sue, and my father, Richard, who gave me my beginning and gave me their image

To my children, Lauren and Rachel, who are my light and the mirror into which I gaze

To my first grandson, Noah, whose natural curiosity and quest for knowledge are inspiring

To my brother, Michael, and sister, Lisa, with whom I climb Jacob's ladder

To my sister, Julia, who has the forceful and courageous spirit of Dinah

To my best friend, David, who in the manner of Joseph, sees my dreams and expands my universe.

To Helen Goldberg, escapee of the Holocaust, whose wisdom and whose great courage during an evil flood are the essence of my Noah

To Judy Wax-Goldwasser, professional writer and elementary through high school classmate, whose passion for my book and keen perceptive suggestions were an invaluable blessing

To Marilyn Green, a friend whose enthusiastic comments made me more secure about publishing this book

CJS

If you have found this book to be thought-provoking...
be provoked some more by visiting my blog.
jigSawpuzzlings.com

CPSIA information can be obtained
at www.ICGtesting.com
Printed in the USA
FSOW01n0536040815
9536FS